AGENT OF CHAOS

AGENT OF CHAOS

—— NORMAN SPINRAD ——

INTRODUCTION BY
BARRY N. MALZBERG

FRANKLIN WATTS   NEW YORK   TORONTO   1988

Library of Congress Catalog Card Number 87-51221
ISBN 0-531-15072-0

Copyright © 1967, 1970, 1988 by Norman Spinrad
Introduction copyright © 1988 by Barry N. Malzberg
Printed in the United States of America
6   5   4   3   2   1

AGENT OF CHAOS

INTRODUCTION BY BARRY N. MALZBERG

Agent of Chaos is Norman Spinrad's second novel, although only by a margin of a few months. (His published first, *The Solarians*, was conceived if not written later.) It is a remarkable work in many regards, not the least of which is that it is perfectly characteristic of the writer and his concerns for the next two decades and counting. Here are all the grand themes: paranoia; society as a perilous accommodation which can and probably *should* be torn apart through the questioning of its assumptions by the powermakers; the powermakers and shufflers themselves portrayed as a group of demented civil servants, ex-bikers, ex-politicians, holy rollers or sword and sorcery writers whose efforts to control all of the others come mostly from digestive problems. Here in this novel are prefigured Spinrad's later works: *The Iron Dream* (Hitler as an exile and writer of barbarian fantasy, pouring the Third Reich into a Hugo winner), *The Mind Game* (social and psychological control as an ultimate put-on by a science fiction writer, the writer's prank against the world), *Bug Jack Barron* (apocalypse as entertainment for the masses), and any number of short stories like "Carcinoma Angels," "The Big Flash," "A Thing of Beauty," in which reality is something of a by-product of combat, a declaration by the winners. ("The National Pastime," about that singular sensation, combat football, is probably the best and purest distillation.)

Many first novels do prefigure a writer's concerns throughout a career; one thinks of *Beautiful and the Damned, Solar Lottery*, or *Catcher in the Rye*. But that is not the most remarkable aspect of this work. What makes it remarkable is not only that the very young writer states explicitly so early in his career its grand theme:

> ". . . Order is logical, Chaos illogical . . . consider the law of Social Entropy . . . the natural tendency in the physical realm is toward ever-increasing randomness or disorder, what we call Chaos or entropy. So too in the realm of human culture. To locally and temporarily reverse the trend towards entropy in the physical realm requires energy. And so too in human societies . . . the more Ordered, thus unnatural, antientropic, a society, the more Social Energy is required to maintain the unnatural condition. And how is this Social Energy to be obtained? Why, by so ordering the society to produce it! Which, as you can see, requires more Order in return. Which creates a demand for more Social Energy . . . the more Ordered a society becomes, the more Ordered it must become to maintain its original Order . . . thus a society can tolerate less and less randomness as it grows ever more ordered . . ."

but also that Spinrad's Brotherhood of Assassins, who act to break down the Hegemony through random, bizarre, extrinsic activities, had a real-life series of disciples. From the late-sixties Yippies of Hoffman and Rubin came the anarchic Zippies of Forcade who adopted Spinradian notions of social overthrow, conducted Be-ins at Grand Central, Fornicationins (this is a euphemism) in Central Park, trash-ins on various commuter lines, and (for a little extra income) pie-in-the-face-ins, a bureaucracy of pie assassinations of victims of choice for fees.

Forcade came to a calamitous end, the Zippies, Yippies, and Hippies may be seen on exhibit with the one and only Billy Shears at Sergeant Pepper's, and notions of social-change-through-entropy have the quaintness to our bleak-but-stiff-upper-lip-now eighties perspective that the songs of Guy Mitchell had to our earlier sixties selves. Yet this novel is being reissued, giving evidence through its very appearance, and at this moment, that something of the social vision here is not only persistent but remains attractive.

The novel, of course, on one level can be seen as other than social documentary: from the perspective of hermetic science-fictionist, possibly Spinrad's self-perception at the time, *Agent of Chaos* is a perfect put-on of all those 1950's science fiction novels he and Cyril Kornbluth and I had read in which the gallant-if-initially-misunderstood Underground brings the brutal Authoritarian-Regime-of-oppressors to its knees. This is the plot that launched more adolescent (and adult) fantasies than we would ever dare admit, and here is Spinrad in 1966 taking a long, hard look at the cliché and intimating that they're *all* crazy, Underground too (but nobody crazier than the fourteen-year-old readers), and the only solution is to get completely outside of the system. As such, as pure science-fiction commentary or *obiter dicta*, this novel makes irresistible sense. Like every good writer, however, and no matter how early, Spinrad put somewhat more into this, perhaps, than he thought. The only question remaining then within the context of an essay published more than two decades after this novel was first delivered to its original publisher is whether *Agent of Chaos* would have been reissued, would have been worth reissuing, if its author had not gone on to a splendid and valuable career, if it had been the only work of a writer never heard from again. Would it have been reissued? I do not think so; the processes of modern publishing, alas, do not work that way; we are not so great on our detritus if it cannot be systematized, granted provenance.

But *should* it, in that hypothetical instance, have been reissued? Most assuredly, yes. Under these or any circumstances we are lucky to have it. This is a relevant and disturbing book; Ching's atomization, his way out of the system that sees only self-obliteration as ecstasy, is terribly American to me, grimly provocative, and it is this—not Zippies, Forcade or social theory—which persists; the splinters and slivers of light as Ching goes up, Ching goes down, all goes up, all goes down and barely a decade now from all millennial prophecies we wriggle, stunned, toward our own Be-In. Our own judgment. Our own agency, discovered chaos, thanks be to the one and only Billy Shears.

New Jersey, 1987

"Every Social Conflict is the arena for three mutually antagonistic forces: the Establishment, the opposition which seeks to overthrow the existing Order and replace it with one of its own, and the tendency towards increased Social Entropy which all Social Conflict engenders, and which, in this context, may be thought of as the force of Chaos."

Gregor Markowitz,
The Theory of Social Entropy

1

Boris Johnson stepped lightly and automatically off the outermost strip of the groundlevel glideway and onto the sidewalk lip. The pristine, cold white bulk of the new Ministry of Guardianship building bulked proud and inhuman in front of him, separated from the groundlevel sidewalk by a broad expanse of lawn which completely ringed the building on groundlevel.

A crowd, if one could call it that, had already been gathered in front of the Ministry steps, at the base of which a small speaker's podium had been set up. Johnson estimated that there were perhaps three to four thousand Wards present: placid, indifferent-looking men and women who had obviously been herded to the Ministry for the occasion by the Guards. They stood and waited, did not chatter among themselves, did not fidget. Like all such gatherings of the Wards of the Hegemony, it was an inert mass of people, rather than a real *crowd*. Johnson noted that the Wards had been confined to a comparatively small, semicircular area whose base was the Ministry steps by a ring of surly looking Guards, scowling like shaved apes stuffed into tuxedos in their seldom-worn dress uniforms. Thus, what people who were present were packed into a tight mass, even though there were still wide expanses of empty lawn available on groundlevel.

So far, so good.

Sauntering slowly, a nonchalance at wild variance with the tension he felt painted on his bluff but not quite hard features, Johnson walked past the ring of Guards at the periphery of the crowd. He passed directly in front of one of the Guards, a big, beefy man, with deep lines of permanent suspicion and hostility etched on his cruel-eyed face. He gave the Guard a casual nod, for he was dressed in the gray coveralls of Ministry Maintenance, and such a gesture was more or less expected. The Guard's face creased in a cold, lizard's smile, and Johnson smiled back, a quick grin of equal sincerity.

As he elbowed his way closer to the speaker's podium, Johnson saw why the Wards had been crowded into such an unnecessarily small space. A television crew had set up their equipment on the secondlevel street—about thirty feet above groundlevel and connected directly to the Ministry by a rampway—and they would be shooting the dedication ceremonies directly over the heads of the crowd, thus giving the illusion of a vast, packed audience surrounding the Ministry.

Johnson snickered to himself, while keeping his features carefully bland. It was typical Hegemonic overcontrol. As he surveyed the setup more closely, he realized that the whole thing was really a carefully designed set for the benefit of the television cameras, which would carry Khustov's speech live to all the domes on Mars, and later, via tape, throughout the Hegemony. It was all planned for effect: the rarely worn, ornate blue, gold, and black dress uniforms of the Guards; the illusion of a vast audience; the sheer, windowless white walls of the Ministry soaring like a huge backdrop screen behind the podium; the large Hegemonic flag—nine concentric gold circles in a field of blue—flapping in the breeze. . . . *Flapping in the breeze?*

Johnson had to fight to keep from laughing. Since every molecule of air in every dome was artificially produced and carefully circulated by the dome's environment control system, there *were* no breezes on Mars to ruffle a flag. Apparently, they had set up a hidden blower behind the flag to create one!

Somehow, it was the perfect final touch.

Just right for the script—a pompous dedication speech for the new Martian Ministry of Guardianship building by the Hegemonic Coordinator himself.

What they don't know, Johnson thought as he casually thrust his hands into his pockets and stroked the barrel of the lasegun under his right hand, is that there has been a small revision written into the script by the Democratic League.

It would be quite a show, all right, if not quite what the Hegemonic Council had planned. Instead, every Ward on Mars (they would, of course, never run the tape on the other planets) would be treated to the public spectacle of the assassination of Vladimir Khustov, the Hegemonic Coordinator himself.

After this, the Democratic League would *have* to be taken seriously. Khustov would be dead, and far too many people would have witnessed the event for the Hegemony to wipe it from the consciousness of the Wards by denying, in the usual fashion, that it had ever happened. Johnson fingered the contents of his left pocket: an annunciator bomb, a small ovoid containing a prerecorded message announcing that the League had assassinated Khustov. After the assassination, it would be released to fly above the crowd on its tiny rotors, broadcasting its message not only to the Wards present in the flesh, but to millions of television sets all over Mars. Every Ward on Mars would know who killed the Coordinator.

The League was so small, and so weak, and against a tyranny like the Hegemony, a tyranny that controlled not only all the inhabited planets and moons of the Solar System but every media of communication as well, it was nearly impossible to even make the League's existence known to a sizeable proportion of the Hegemony's populace.

It took a lot more than planning to accomplish anything of significance—it took large doses of luck.

Luck that the Hegemonic Council had decided to televise the dedication ceremonies.

And even greater luck that Arkady Solkowni had joined the League on his own initiative.

Johnson craned his neck above the crowd and surveyed the Guards stationed around the periphery. Uniformly big men, uniformly sullen and suspicious, their laseguns at the ready, their eyes constantly scanning the crowd. They eyed each other with even greater suspicion, a suspicion born of carefully nurtured and conditioned paranoia.

The Guards were carefully picked men, thoroughly screened and conditioned. They had to have just the right family background, psychological profile, school record, even genetic traits. And even once their backgrounds passed muster, they were put through a solid week of depth interrogation under a whole battery of psychodrugs.

It was utterly impossible for League agents to infiltrate the Guards. No amount of dedication, skill or planning could accomplish it.

Only luck.

No League agent could become a Guard, but it was not totally impossible for a Guard to become a member of the League, as Arkady Solkowni had. And Solkowni was not only a Guard, he was a member of Khustov's personal bodyguard.

Yes, luck was one of the few remaining factors that the Hegemony had not yet found a way to control. So they compensated for it. The Guards were potentially the weak point in the Hegemony's iron control of the Solar System, and the Council had long been aware of the danger. Submissiveness, apathy, bovine indifference, were ideal traits in a controlled populace—and the Wards moved further in that direction every day—but they would be intolerable in the paramilitary organization designed to control that populace. The Guards had to be alert, ruthless, possessed of considerable initiative, and tough.

In a word, it was necessary that they be *dangerous.*

But one thing the Hegemony could not tolerate was a tough, armed elite group of men with an internal esprite, a Praetorian Guard.

Wasn't it one of the old suppressed philosophers, Plato or Toynbee or Markowitz, Johnson thought, who had posed that old paradox: "Who shall guard the Guardians"?

Johnson grimaced inwardly. Whoever he was, he had not lived under the Hegemony! The Hegemony had the answer. . . .

The answer was fear. Institutionalized and carefully created paranoia. *The Guards* guarded the Guards. They were conditioned to distrust every human being but the Councilors themselves; they watched each other with even greater suspicion than that with which they watched the Wards. They were deliberately trained to be trigger-happy—as the Preamble to the Revised Hegemonic Constitution said, "Better a million Wards shall perish than one Unpermitted Act go unpunished." The Guards were more like a pack of intelligent but ill-tamed hunting dogs than an army. They were conditioned to kill anyone that seemed the least bit out of line, and that included their own pack brothers.

Paradoxically, it was this very institutionalized paranoia that brought a man like Solkowni to doubt the Hegemonic Council itself, and to transfer his one remaining loyalty at least temporarily to the Democratic League. It does not take much to turn a "one man dog" into a "no man dog."

At any rate, Johnson thought, no one Guard could assassinate Khustov. The others in the bodyguard would gleefully cut him down the moment he made a suspicious move.

Unless. . . .

Johnson studied the blank, vacant faces of the Wards pressed close about him. Fear, prosperity, and iron control were enabling the Hegemony to reduce the Wards to nothing more than well-fed, well-housed, well-amused domestic cattle. They lacked nothing but freedom, and the very meaning of that word was rapidly becoming obscure.

Four thousand Wards of the Hegemony—human cattle, totally harmless in themselves. But scattered among that apathetic herd were ten armed League agents, ten killers.

By themselves, the ten agents could not kill Khustov. Among other things, Guards were required to be unnaturally big men—none of them were under six foot six. Khustov would be surrounded by a ring of Guards, and at the slightest hint of trouble, they would form a shield around him with their own bodies.

The agents in the crowd could not kill Khustov. Solkowni could not kill Khustov. The Wards would never dream of killing Khustov.

But all three together. . . .

Now there was a stir by the arched entranceway at the top of the Ministry steps. Eight burly Guards in dress uniforms emerged from the building—Khustov's personal bodyguard. The blond one at the extreme right would be Arkady Solkowni.

Boris Johnson checked his watch. The television coverage should be just starting now, and any second Khustov would appear.

There was a blare of recorded trumpets from the podium itself, and Vladimir Khustov, the Hegemonic Coordinator, appeared at the top of the steps, barely visible behind the screen of Guards.

Khustov marched slowly down the steps, screened always by the Guards, as the notes of "Nine Planets Forever," the Hegemonic Anthem, filled the air.

Johnson had never seen Khustov in the flesh before, though of course his television image was all too familiar to everyone in the Hegemony. Though Johnson himself would not have cared to admit it, there was a curious resemblance between the Hegemonic Coordinator and himself—though a resemblance blurred by a fifty-year age difference. Both had long, straight black hair, and if Khustov's had been thinned by his eighty years, the fact was artfully concealed. Johnson had the chunky body of an athlete; Khustov looked like a long-retired boxer—heavy muscles long since gone to fat. Both men had gray eyes, and if Johnson's were mercurial while Khustov's were iron-cold, they both had a curious sense of aliveness all too rare in common Wards of the Hegemony.

Khustov and his bodyguards reached the podium at the foot of the steps. The Coordinator was standing directly behind the podium as the last notes of the Anthem were played. Four of the Guards hunkered on a little platform that projected out from the front of the podium, in position to shield Khustov from the crowd instantly, by simply standing up. The other four Guards had split into two pairs, one to either side of Khustov and slightly behind him one step up from the podium.

Solkowni was the inside man in the right-hand pair behind the podium. Another piece of good luck.

The music stopped.

"Wards of the Hegemony . . ." Khustov began, in English. Although his name was Russian, Khustov's ancestry was known to be at least half American, and he was quite fluent in both official languages, Russian and English. Since Mars was largely American-settled, he had chosen to speak in English, as Johnson had anticipated.

It was important to the plan that all eleven of the League agents open fire within a few seconds of each other. Since they were scattered throughout the crowd, there was no way that Johnson could give a secure signal. Therefore, it had been arbitrarily decided that they would open fire the first time that Khustov said the word "Guardianship." Since it was the new Ministry of Guardianship building that was being dedicated, and since Khustov was speaking in English, it was a safe assumption that he would use the word sooner or later.

Johnson tightened his grip on the lasegun in his pocket. This was really it, the first real step toward the destruction of the Hegemony and the restoration of Democracy. The death of Khustov as such did not really matter—Jack Torrence, the Vice-Coordinator, would speedily use the opportunity to seize and consolidate power—but the fact that the Democratic League *could* kill a Coordinator would at long last make it a force to be reckoned with, after ten years of futile, furtive meetings, subrosa word of mouth propaganda and very minor sabotage.

". . . and so another brick in the great edifice of Order is being placed today . . ." Khustov droned on. ". . . another bulwark in the defense against chaos, disorder, and the hunger, discontent and unhappiness that such social strife brings. Yes, Wards of the Hegemony, this great new Ministry building will enable the Mars Division of the Ministry of Guardianship to improve upon even—"

Guardianship!

Johnson drew his lasegun. The compact weapon—with its translucent sythruby barrel jutting out of the six-inch black ebonite handle which contained the standard magazine holding fifty tiny electrocrystals each of which would give up the stored energy in its structure in one terrific burst of coherent light when the button trigger was pressed—could not be mistaken for anything innocuous. At Johnson's right, a fat woman screamed shrilly. The man with her tried desperately to push through the solid wall of people to safety. In seconds, all the Wards within sight of Johnson were frantically trying to bull their way through their neighbors to escape the obvious madman.

But they got nowhere, for now ten similar "madmen" within the crowd were also the foci of pushing knots of Wards, and the crazed Wards were shoving insanely against each other in their fear, preventing anyone from escaping.

Johnson pointed his lasegun outward, at the ring of Guards containing the crowd, pressed the trigger. A powerful beam of coherent light flashed from the barrel as the electrocrystal in the chamber gave up its energy and crumbled to dust.

The beam seared into the shoulder of a hulking, darkskinned Guard. He screamed, writhed in pain, and fired instantly with his good right arm back in the general direction of Johnson. A Ward was hit and began to scream. Soon there were dozens, scores, hundreds of Wards screaming in terror and confusion.

As soon as he had fired, Boris Johnson had bulldozed his way closer to the podium. He fired again, this time in the general direction of the podium itself. Khustov's bodyguards had already formed a tight circle, behind which the Coordinator crouched, all but invisible. Johnson's shot touched the plastomarble steps near the podium, melting a small area of the synthetic into a viscous puddle which slowly began to dribble down the steps.

As he paused to sight for another shot, Johnson saw that his men were also doing their jobs. One of them had hit the flag, and the remains of it flaked from the flagpole, black, burnt-out ash. As he watched, a lasebeam sizzled through the bottom of the flagpole, and the pole tottered for a brief moment before falling across the podium, narrowly missing Khustov.

The crowd was now in an advanced state of panic. Individual Wards raced around in mad circles, blindly pushing, kicking, screaming. Here and there a few Wards formed a wedge, tried to fight their way outward, but the Guards at the periphery of the crowd were firing, and so the wedges were hurled back by hordes of Wards just as frantically trying to escape the inward fire of the Guards. The crowd stampeded about mindlessly, like cattle before a prairie fire.

Johnson aimed a shot well wide of the human wall of Guard surrounding Khustov—it was, of course, essential that none of the League agents hit Solkowni by mistake.

The air was filled with screams and shouts, with the acrid smells of charred flesh, seared metal, melted synthetic. The Guards containing the crowd could do nothing effective— the League agents who were doing the shooting were effectively hidden in the panic-stricken mob milling all around them. But that did not stop the Guards from reacting as their conditioning and training demanded. They emptied their guns in the general direction of where they imagined League agents to be, savagely indifferent to the fact that they were only slaughtering hapless Wards. They were like dogs in a henhouse: they were after the foxes, and it didn't much matter how many of the chickens they were supposed to be protecting perished in the hunt.

Three lasebeams, in rapid succession, lanced into the same section of Guards at the periphery in a tight pattern. Two of them went down, and the others answered with a terrible fusilade of concentrated fire into a small area of the crowd. A great piteous moan went up from the Wards as they suddenly realized that the Guards were beginning to *enjoy* the excuse for carnage.

All according to plan. . . . Johnson thought triumphantly. Soon even Khustov's personal bodyguards will stop thinking and start killing for kicks, and then none of 'em'll notice when Solkowni. . . .

Now!

"Let's get out! Let's get out!" Johnson began to scream rhythmically. "To the street! To the street!"

And as they had planned, the other League agents took up the same chant, and in moments the Wards themselves were picking up the cry, down to the pounding, urgent rhythm of it.

"Over there!" cried Johnson, shoving the man in front of him. "Look, a break in their ranks! Let's get out!"

Suddenly, a great wave cresting, the entire crowd of terror-maddened Wards broke and ran, a headlong, mindless charge, straight at the line of Guards cordoning them off from the street and safety. The apathetic, placid Wards of the Hegemony had been galvanized by fear into a savage mob.

Not fear, but feral bloodlust lit the gleaming eyes of the Guards as they braced against the charge. It was savage against savage, but the savages in the gaudy dress uniforms had the guns. They began firing into the mob at pointblank range. The massed lasegun fire of the Guards met the forward edge of the mob like a wall of flame. Scores of Wards screamed, blackened and fell.

Almost instantly, the charge broke and the panic returned and the Wards reversed themselves, began to rush blindly back toward the Ministry steps, where Khustov's personal bodyguards awaited them with guns and animal fury.

This should be it! Johnson thought.

The bodyguards began firing into the mob, feral glazed eyes fixed hypnotically on their victims. Khustov himself crouched safely behind their great bodies, apparently secure in the knowledge that the unarmed Wards would never be able to breach the human wall surrounding him.

Seven of the Guards fired away mercilessly at the onrushing Wards, and now the charge began to falter in the face of their withering fire as Ward after Ward was charred into ruined ash. . . .

But the eighth Guard suddenly swiveled around and trained the barrel of his lasegun directly on Coordinator Khustov's head. The other Guards were too engrossed in the slaughter before them to notice what was going on behind.

The plan was working! In another second—

But as Johnson watched in numb, mute amazement, Solkowni's body was hit by at least five separate lasebeams, all but simultaneously, before he could fire. He had but a moment to stare stupidly upward as his whole body was crisped to ashes in less than a second. The husk of his body remained blackened and upright for a moment, then collapsed in a decomposing heap.

What in hell happened? Johnson thought wildly, too stunned to yet feel disappointment. That was no fluke. . . . Then he glanced upward, at the secondlevel street where six men were dashing past the dumfounded television crew towards the secondlevel glideway. . . .

Khustov had screamed, and the Guards had whirled to stare woodenly at the heap of ashes on the steps.

"Up the steps, you cretins!" Khustov roared, his face livid with rage and fear. Encircled by his now wary bodyguards, the Hegemonic Coordinator retreated safely up the steps.

The six running men on the secondlevel street reached the glideway just as Khustov was about to enter the Ministry.

Just before he stepped on the outer glideway strip to be whisked away to relative safety, the last man tossed something rounded and silvery into the air.

A bomb? Johnson thought dazedly.

But then he could see the tiny rotors holding the bomb in the air as it flew low over the crowd. It was a bomb, all right, an annunciator-bomb. But annunciator-bombs were only used by the Democratic League! The League, and—

"Coordinator Khustov's life," boomed the hollow, amplified voice of the annunciator bomb, "has been saved, courtesy of the Brotherhood of Assassins."

*"In a place with no past there is nowhere
to conceal the future from the present."*

Gregor Markowitz,
Chaos And Culture

2

Boris Johnson tossed his lasegun away into the crowd, half out of disgust, half as an automatic precaution—Khustov was safe, and now the lasegun could only serve to identify him as one of the would-be assassins. It looked as if the other League agents were doing the same, for now the only firing was coming from the cordon of Guards, and in a few moments even they realized that whatever had happened was over, and they too ceased firing.

The Guards tightened up their cordon, forced the now-quieting crowd closer back against the Ministry steps, held the Wards within a firm semicircle of guns. They seemed to be waiting for someone or something. . . .

The Brotherhood of Assassins!, Johnson thought with almost petulant bitterness as he felt for the false identity papers in his pocket. Why? What had made the Brotherhood save Khustov?

But then, who really knew *anything* of real significance about the Brotherhood? The Brotherhood of Assassins was supposed to have come into being three hundred years ago, at about the same time that the American-dominated Atlantic Union had merged with the Greater Soviet Union to form the Hegemony of Sol.

In the beginning, the Brotherhood had seemed to be some sort of resistance movement. They had assassinated three out of the first seven Hegemonic Coordinators. They had killed something like a score of Councilors. They had planted the fusion bomb which destroyed Port Gagarin.

But after a decade or so, the pattern of Brotherhood activity seemed to have become insane. They saved the Umbriel colony when a freak meteor storm holed the dome, but then they turned around and blew open the dome on Ceres, murdering the entire population of the only inhabited asteroid. They began killing Wards, seemingly at random as well as Hegemonic officials and Guards. There was no logical pattern—it was as if they were followers of some archaic cult from the Millennium of Religion, some superstitious dogma with no meaning for the uninitiated.

And now, for no visible reason, they had saved Khustov.

An aircar landed just outside the ring of Guards, and a man stepped out, dressed in the plain green fatigues that the Guards normally wore. But he was not the ordinary huge, tough-looking Guard. He was short, slight, almost whispy, and there was an abstracted, far-away look to his pale blue eyes.

Johnson grimaced, for this was exactly what he had feared the most—they had brought in an Edetic.

Johnson was carrying two sets of forged identity papers. One set was for "Samuel Sklar," a merchant who had a travel pass from Earth to Phobos and back. "Sklar" could never officially be on Mars. While on Mars, Johnson was "Vassily Thomas," a Maintenance worker in the Ministry of Guardianship. Thus, even if Johnson's presence on Mars should be discovered, the Guards would be searching for "Thomas," while once back on Phobos, Johnson would be home free as "Sklar," who would never have even been on Mars.

But now all bets were off.

For the frail-looking Guard who had just arrived was an Edetic, a man with a carefully selected and conditioned faculty for total recall. He would have memorized the complete description of every Hegemonic Enemy, and no such Enemy, no matter how good his papers, could fool the Edetic's photographic memory.

And Boris Johnson, as head of the Democratic League, was Hegemonic Enemy Number One.

Now Johnson saw what the Guards were doing. They were slowly and methodically passing the Wards out of the cordon, one by one past the unblinking gaze of the Edetic. It would take hours to let all the Wards out at this rate, but the Guards had all the time in the world, and since no one could leave without passing the Edetic, they could be sure that they would capture every one of the League agents.

Johnson knew that there was no safe way past the Edetic.

But maybe. . . . Johnson could not help smiling, despite his predicament. Where was the last place the Guards would look for a Hegemonic Enemy but in their own headquarters! Which was what the Ministry of Guardianship really was. The new Mars Master Guardian, the central computer for the whole planet, was buried somewhere in the bowels of the Ministry, but the rest of the building served as headquarters for the Martian Guards. If he could somehow get up the steps and into the building. . . . Well, there would be problems enough once inside, but at least he would escape the Edetic.

Using knees and elbows, Johnson made his way through the crowd to the podium at the foot of the steps. With the sour air of Maintenance men since time immemorial surveying such messes, he bent down and prodded the fused metal and melted plastomarble at the base of the podium.

As he saw a scowling Guard approach, he began to curse and mumble loudly to himself. "Damned thing is fused solid! Damn filthy mess! Take five hours to—"

"What do you think *you're* doing?" barked the Guard, training his lasegun on Johnson.

"What am I doing? What kind of stupid question is that? Maybe you think I can clean up this mess with my bare hands? This is a real bitch here! It's fused solid, man! Take a torch to cut it loose, and a thermogun to reform the plastomarble. A half-day's work at least!"

"Maintenance jerks!" the Guard grunted. "Don't just squat there looking stupid! Get to work on this mess!"

"*Told* you," Johnson whined. "Can't very well do anything without a torch and a thermogun."

"Well then why in blazes don't you go and get 'em?" bellowed the Guard.

"You fellas seem to be keeping everyone out of the building," Johnson muttered, sullenly triumphant.

The Guard shook his head knowingly. "You slobs'll use any excuse to get out of doing a little work!" he said. "Now you drag your tail up into the Ministry and get your torch and thermogun and get to work on this, and you do it *now!*"

"No need to get excited," Johnson whined with the wounded expression of the apprehended goldbricker. "I'm going, I'm going."

He climbed up the Ministry steps under the flinty stare of the Guard and entered the building through the service entrance, a small doorway to the left of the great arched entranceway.

As he stepped inside, he permitted himself one small laugh; there would be no opportunity for gloating inside the Ministry. The halls here, as in every other public building, and an ever-increasing number of private ones, were filled with Beams and Eyes. It was said that even the wrong expression on your face could mean instant and certain death.

The door opened directly into the main lobby. Since the building had just been officially opened, the lobby was virtually empty except for a few scattered Guards, who were accustomed to looking through Maintenance personnel as if they weren't there.

The escape route was simple—about fifty yards across the lobby to the bank of elevators, take an elevator to the third floor, and then leave the building through the second-level street exit. Once on the secondlevel street glideway, Johnson knew he would be far away from the Ministry in minutes. Surely the few Guards in the building would not notice the comings and goings of a mere Maintenance man. . . .

Nevertheless, Johnson's palms were clammy with fear as he started across the lobby, for he had not gone ten feet when he had to pass the first Eye. The Eye was deceptively inconspicuous—nothing but the small glass lens of a television pickup set flush with the wall and the even smaller grid of a microphone directly behind it. The camera and mike fed directly into the Mars Master Guardian, the great computer which administered the Code of Justice locally. The Prime Directive programmed into the Guardian was, so it was said, "Anything not Permitted is Prohibited." What this was supposed to mean in practice was that the rest of the Hegemonic Code was a long list of what a Ward *could* do in a given area, so-called Permitted Actions. Anything which did not fit the list of Permitted Actions programmed into the Guardian was an Unpermitted Action—a *crime*. All crimes were punishable by death.

And trial, sentence and execution were instantaneous.

Directly below the Eye was a tiny lead plug, also set flush with the wall. This plug sealed a lead cylinder, a Beam, which was recessed within the wall and which contained a deadly radioactive isotope. The Beams too were circuited directly into the nearest Guardian.

Thus, "Justice" had been reduced by the Hegemony to an automatic reflex arc. An Eye continuously fed observations into the nearest Guardian and the Guardian continuously checked the data against its list of Permitted Actions. It was said that if any action, no matter how trivial, proved to be Unpermitted, a signal automatically went to the Beam below the Eye that had reported it. The lead plug was blown out, and the area filled with deadly radiation. The reaction time of the system was under one second. Whether it was really true, that the Guardian would kill a man for any Unpermitted Action, that such a program could actually be put into a computer, Johnson did not know. But he did know that many, many Wards had died in seemingly innocent circumstances. . . .

Johnson passed the first Eye and noted somewhat distantly that he was still alive. If what the Hegemony said about the Beam and Eyes was true, then it would be so easy to make a fatal mistake—a rebellious look, an item of non-standard equipment, a blunder into some zone where Maintenance personnel were not supposed to go. The hell of it was that the number of actions which would *not* cause the Guardian to pop a plug was quite finite, while the actions that *would* result in death were literally infinite in number. And if the Hegemony was lying about the Guardian, it was even worse, for then death might come for no reason at all!

The Beams and Eyes were spotted at ten foot intervals, which meant that he would have to pass five of them before he reached the elevators. One was already past; now he passed another, with a studied air of casual indifference that he hoped was not too exaggerated—for attempting to fool an Eye would be in itself an Unpermitted Action!

The Beams and Eyes were in virtually every public building in the Hegemony: stores, theaters, flics as well as government buildings. Just about everywhere indoors—the radiation from the Beams would tend to scatter too much outdoors and the "criminals" would have a decent chance to flee as the plug was popped—except in private residences. And there was a rumor going around that the Council was about to decide to install Beams and Eyes in all new dwellings. If it were true, it would mean the end of just about the last bit of privacy a Ward could know. . . .

Johnson passed the third Eye . . . the fourth. . . . Now there was only one Eye between him and the elevators. It was located right above the bank of three elevators, apparently so that it could prevent unauthorized personnel from using them. This would be the trickiest part of all. . . .

As he approached the middle elevator, Johnson took a rag out of a coverall pocket. Humming to himself, he began to polish the brass fittings outside the open elevator. Then, with the polishing rag still in his hand, he casually stepped inside and immediately began polishing the inside doorhandle.

I'm still alive! he thought triumphantly. It's working!

Then, as he was about to reach out and push the button

for the third floor, he happened to glance upward, and his heart sank.

There was a Beam and an Eye in the ceiling of the elevator!

There's got to be a way to. . . . It's risky, he thought, but I've got no choice.

He finished shining up the doorhandle and began to polish the small console of floor buttons. As he passed the rag over the buttons, he pushed "three" with his thumb, through the rag.

As the door closed and the elevator began to rise, he jumped backward in what he hoped was well-feigned surprise. Then he shrugged, and went on with his polishing. He held his breath for long moments as the elevator rose. . . .

The Eye was fooled. The Beam's plug didn't pop!

The elevator stopped at the third floor and the door opened. Johnson gave the button console a final touch with his polishing rag and then stepped casually out of the elevator.

As he made his way down the corridor to the secondlevel street exit, he suppressed a sigh of relief. It was working. The worst was over. Apparently not even the Guardian itself took much notice of the puttering of a Maintenance man!

After traversing what seemed like a mile long corridor under the scrutiny of what seemed like a million Eyes, Johnson finally found himself outside the Ministry on the short ramp that led from the building to the secondlevel street. If he could get to the street itself without being noticed, he could simply skip across the accelerating strips of the glideway to the central express strip and be whisked miles away in minutes, hidden amidst crowds of Wards. . . .

Johnson began walking briskly but not too hurriedly across the ramp to the secondlevel street. A few more yards, and . . .

"Hey you!" bellowed a voice from the groundlevel street below.

Johnson looked down. It was a Guard. "You, up there!"

the Guard shouted. "Back in the building! No one leaves this area yet!"

Johnson took a few steps back towards the Ministry, positioning himself in the center of the ramp as he did so, where the ramp itself would give him some cover from lasebeams from below. Suddenly he whirled around and broke into a dead run towards the glideway.

It was only a matter of a few yards, a second or two. The Guards below got off two shots which weren't even close, and then Johnson was at the lip of the glideway. He leapt onto the two-mile-an-hour outermost strip of the glideway, bowling over a fat man who waved his fist foolishly as Johnson skipped inward, onto the seven-mile-an-hour strip.

Already, he was several blocks from the Ministry. The important thing now was not to raise too much of a stir; the glideway was filled with Wards, and a man rushing around bowling them over would stand out like a spider in an anthill. Forcing himself to be leisurely about it, Johnson made his way inward toward the thirty-mile-an-hour express strip, threading his way politely through the Wards on the twelve, eighteen and twenty-five-mile-an-hour strips.

Finally, he was standing on the express strip itself. He had bought some time, but not very much. Within an hour, maybe less, all Guards would be alerted to be on the watch for a man in Maintenance coveralls answering the description on "Vassily Thomas" papers.

He had to get out of the dome fast, and back to Phobos. He knew that he had at best a few hours of safety left on Mars—and maybe a good deal less than that.

But "Samuel Sklar" would be safe on Phobos.

If Johnson could get out of the dome before they caught up to him.

The iron control of the Hegemony was based on three independent control systems: the Eyes and Beams of the Guardians, the human Guards, and the pass system.

Every Ward was required to carry his personal identity papers with him at all times. In order to travel between the planets and moons, a Ward had to have a specific travel pass for a specific destination attached to his papers. Travel passes were issued only for what the Hegemony considered good reason, and they were valid for a limited time only. There was no such thing as a permanent travel pass, or one good for all planets and moons—except for very high Hegemony officials. Each pass was good for one round trip between two given bodies—unless it was an immigration pass.

Being caught in transit without the proper pass was, like all other Unpermitted Actions, punishable by death.

Johnson had traveled from Earth to Phobos, Mars' great "natural space station," on his "Samuel Sklar" papers, which included a travel pass from Earth to Phobos, with a side jaunt to Deimos permitted. "Vassily Thomas' " papers were for a Martian resident and included no travel passes.

In this way, Johnson was "Thomas" on Mars and "Sklar" while in transit, and there was no traceable connection between the two.

The catch was getting from Phobos to Mars and back illegally.

Johnson had doubled back and changed directions several times along the glideway system to make doubly sure he had lost all pursuit, and was now on a groundlevel express strip, speeding out toward the circumference of the environment dome and airlock eight.

As the buildings whipped by, and the base of the dome came ever closer, Boris Johnson felt that old, familiar *confined* sensation that haunted him everywhere but on Earth.

The trouble with the Extra-Terrestrial Bodies was that all the colonies were islands of Hegemonic control in deadly, hostile environments. Nowhere in the Solar System but Earth could a man survive for a minute without the protection of either a spacesuit or a permaglaze environment dome.

And the domes had all been built by the Hegemony. They were all planned and controlled down to the last molecule of air. It was an ironic paradox—space, the frontier worlds and moons, where all the thinkers of the prespace past had assumed that the traditional freedom of the frontier would reign, were actually the bastions of most total Hegemonic control. On Earth, with its thousands of years of history, its still-remaining areas of wilderness, its secret and forgotten places, millennial accumulations of ruins, there was still some chance to escape temporarily from the Eyes of the Hegemony.

But the colonies were created whole by the Hegemony. The great permaglaze domes that kept death out were like aquariums for tropical fish—or cages.

And so, whatever precarious refuge there was for the Democratic League, it had to be on Earth.

Now Johnson made his way outward, across the decelerating strips of the glideway to the two-mile-an-hour strip adjacent to the lip. He hopped off the glideway and onto the immobile walkway of the street as the 'way passed airlock eight.

Airlock eight was a little-used lock. It was designated as an excursion lock for Martian residents, and since curiosity was a trait that was discouraged, and since there was really very little of interest to anyone but specialists on the Martian surface anyway, the airlock was nearly nonfunctional and only perfunctorily guarded.

And the single Guard slouching by the rack of spacesuits' in front of the outer airlock door looked very, very bored.

Johnson sauntered up to the Guard.

"I'd like to go outside," he said.

"Why?" snapped the big Guard, apparently grateful to have someone to be nasty to.

"Just feel like looking around. Maybe I'll find the Lost City of the Martians," Johnson said, with a little laugh. The Lost City was a standard local joke on Mars, since the closest thing to "Martians" were the little belly-crawling sandtoads.

"Very funny," said the Guard. "But it just so happens that no one's being allowed out of the dome right now."

"Oh. . . ?" said Johnson. "Something wrong?"

"*Something wrong?* Where you been? The Brotherhood of Assassins just tried to kill the Coordinator!"

"The Brotherhood . . . ?" Johnson blurted in amazement. "Why—"

He stopped himself just in time. That damned Khustov was clever, all right! No way to deny that there had been an assassination attempt—all of Mars had seen it—but they must have stopped the television coverage before the Brotherhood annunciator bomb had gone off. It sure looked better for Khustov to have escaped a Brotherhood plot than for the Wards to know that he had been saved from the League by the Brotherhood. Only the few thousand Wards who had been present in the flesh knew what had really happened, and it would be their unaided voices against the full weight of all the mass media. The League assassination attempt, for all that the average Ward of the Hegemony would ever know, had never happened. Damn! Damn! Damn!

"You look kinda funny. . ." said the Guard, fingering his lasegun and eyeing Johnson narrowly.

Johnson thought feverishly. If he didn't get back to Phobos soon, he was a dead man. He had been spotted leaving the Ministry, and any moment now this Guard could get a call and be ordered to stop anyone in Maintenance coveralls answering the general description of "Thomas"—Johnson. If he did that, they would run a general identity check on Thomas' papers. The forged papers were perfect, but if they were checked against the records of the Mars Master Guardian, it would be discovered that "Vassily Thomas" did not exist—there would be no birth record, no school record, no work record, *nothing*. Johnson knew he had to get to Phobos or die, and to get to Phobos, he had to get past this Guard. *Now!*

"There must be some connection. . ." Johnson muttered.

"What"?

"I said there must be some connection," Johnson said. "Between the assassination attempt and the sabotaged spacesuits."

"What're you talking about"? grunted the Guard.

"Well, since you have your orders, I suppose I'll have

to tell you," Johnson said grudgingly. "I'm with suit Maintenance. A couple days ago, we discovered three sabotaged spacesuits at airlock two. Neat job—just some tiny holes in 'em, not large enough to be noticed until you're too far from the dome to get back alive. That's the real reason I wanted to go outside. We're checking all the suits in the dome, but it's a slow job, and we have orders to keep it quiet. It'd be a real mess if the Wards found out that someone had been able to sabotage the suits. Since I can't go outside, I'll have to check 'em right here. Of course, all this is to go no further."

"I know how to maintain security!" snapped the Guard. "Go ahead, check the suits."

Johnson ambled over to the rack of spacesuits and began poring over them. He removed the helmet from one of the suits and stuck his head inside.

"Of all the—!" he suddenly exclaimed, and began cursing long and loud.

"What is it?"

Johnson whistled, withdrew his head from the wide, open collar of the spacesuit. "Man, you just wouldn't believe it!" he said dazedly. "You just wouldn't believe it!"

"What did you find, man?" snapped the Guard.

Johnson pointed numbly into the suit. "Just look at that!" he shrilled. "Just look at it!"

The Guard muttered, loped over to the open spacesuit, stuck his head inside.

Johnson brought the edge of his right hand down hard on the base of the Guard's skull.

The Guard grunted softly and collapsed.

Quickly, Johnson donned a suit. He grabbed up the Guard's lasegun and shot the other suits full of holes.

He paused, stared for a long moment at the unconscious Guard. He knew that the smart thing to do would be to kill the Guard, but somehow he could not bring himself to kill a helpless man, even a pig like this who he would ordinarily shoot with no regret whatever. With a shrug at his own softness, he opened the airlock door and stepped inside.

He hoped that when they found the ruined spacesuits and the unconscious Guard, they would take it for a crude act of terrorism, at least until the Guard was able to talk. After all, this airlock led nowhere but to the empty Martian surface. All interplanetary ships were controlled by the Hegemony—they surely wouldn't take this for what it was: an escape from Mars itself. At least not for a while.

And even later, there would be nothing to link it to "Samuel Sklar," a man who had never been on Mars.

Anyone stumbling across the little ship hidden in the jumble of big, red iron oxide boulders would be hard put indeed to explain its presence on the Martian surface—for it was a simple, tiny Deimos scooter with only enough power to travel between Phobos and Deimos, Mars' miniscule moons.

Boris Johnson scrambled clumsily between the rocks in his bulky spacesuit, and he was breathing hard by the time he had opened the hatch on the little cabin of the scooter. He had been traveling overland as fast as he could, cursing himself all the while for his failure to buy more time by killing the Guard. If they put two and two together before he got the scooter off Mars. . . .

It pleased the Hegemony to maintain as many illusions of freedom as possible. Along with the spiraling prosperity, it helped to keep the Wards placid. Deimos was maintained as a kind of national park, where a man could be alone with the stars on the little airless rock and feel that he was free.

But like all other "freedoms" in the Hegemony, it was pure illusion. Visitors to Phobos were allowed to rent the little Deimos scooters from private agencies. The scooters had just enough power to get from Phobos to Deimos and back again. A man in a scooter might *feel* that the wide void was his to explore, but the hard reality was that he could go nowhere but to Deimos and back again.

Thus the Hegemony felt perfectly secure in letting Wards take scooter-jaunts by themselves—Deimos was a tiny, uninhabited, airless rock, and the scooters carried only a two-day air supply.

"Samuel Sklar" had rented such a scooter on Phobos, from "Phobos Phil," one of the smaller rental agencies. Officially Sklar was now on Deimos—a perfect cover story. And "Phobos Phil" was a member of the League. . . .

Johnson squirmed through the hatch and into the little cabin. The scooter was crude, cheap, and simple: a tiny one-man cabin, which could be sealed airtight, but which had no airlock, since the air loss from opening it directly to the vacuum of space would be minimal; and a cluster of rockets below the cabin, shielded by a sheet-metal shroud.

But Phobos Phil had made some changes in this particular scooter. Externally, it appeared to be an ordinary Deimos scooter, but the shroud concealed far more powerful engines than a scooter was authorized to have. Powerful enough, and with enough extra fuel, so that it could touch down on Mars and get back to Phobos again. . . .

Johnson settled himself in the crude pilot's seat, and then remembered to disconnect the meter. The scooters were rented partly on a mileage basis, and the total mileage of a trip appeared on the scooter's meter—yet another way the Hegemony made sure that a scooter wasn't being used for unauthorized trips.

Johnson punched a button marked "three" on the scooter's little minicomputer. "Three" was the preprogrammed emergency course to Deimos—maximum acceleration all the way.

He braced himself for the blast, and for the hairy trip to come—the idea was to get to Deimos, where the scooter was supposed to be, in the shortest elapsed time possible, thus minimizing the chances of detection.

The rockets cut in with a deafening roar and slammed Johnson down into the seat. It would be six gees all the way to Deimos, without antigravs, without a Gee-Cocoon, but the cruelest part of the trip was that Johnson knew he would have no control over whether he lived or died until the scooter reached Deimos. If it was spotted on this unauthorized course by a Hegemonic ship or detection station, it would be blasted without warning and he would never know what hit him. . . .

As the gees fuzzed his vision, Johnson realized that this was his first moment of repose of any kind since the assassination attempt. He did not welcome it, for now the full weight of the failure pressed upon him, heavier than the six-gee acceleration. The whole plot had been a catastrophe, a total loss. Not only had Khustov escaped, but the Democratic League hadn't even been implicated in the attempt on his life. Putting the blame on the Brotherhood neatly removed the event from the realm of Hegemonic failure, for the attitude of the average Ward toward the Brotherhood was akin to his attitude toward fate or mental illness. Its every action seemed to be the work of insane religious fanatics, following, so it was rumored, the dictates of some superstitious book of arcane mysticism, variously called "The Bible" or "The Koran" or "The Theory of Social Entropy."

No one seemed to know what was in this book, but whatever it was, it was something straight out of the Millennium of Religion, and as such, the madmen who worshipped it could only be regarded as a natural nuisance—like some of the other mental illnesses which still persisted.

Which made it very convenient for the Council to pin League actions on the Brotherhood of Assassins, and thus dismiss them as simply the work of madmen. . . .

Johnson strained his eyes to read the chronometer. Only another minute or so to Deimos. . . .

Maybe I'll make it after all . . . he thought. Whatever good *that'll* do. . . . The cold truth was that the League was getting nowhere. Membership, small to begin with, was declining. And Hegemonic control grew ever tighter. More and more places were being equipped with Eyes and Beams. The Wards became ever more cowlike and contented as the living standard soared and the punishment for Unpermitted Actions became more and more certain.

And now the Brotherhood too seemed to be somehow aiding the Hegemony, however inadvertently. . . .

Or was the Brotherhood of Assassins a creature of the Hegemony in the first place?

Maybe there was no point in going on. . . . Maybe the most merciful thing would be for the scooter to be detected, and . . .

Just then, the rockets cut out. Johnson floated in the seat straps, suddenly weightless. And even as the end of the acceleration eased the weight of his body, the sight of Deimos, that dead, jagged rock hanging outside the viewport, eased his spirit.

Whatever else had happened, at least he was alive. He had made it to Deimos, and now he was home free. Now he was "Samuel Sklar," returning to Phobos from a jaunt to Deimos. In minutes, he would be back on Phobos, and in a day he would be aboard a ship for Earth, the one place where the League at least had a fighting chance to survive. Two thousand of the League's three thousand members were on Earth.

Earth was still too complex, too honeycombed with forgotten places, to be totally controlled. The League survived, and he survived. A battle had been lost, but the fight would go on, the fight to destroy the Hegemony and replace it with that thing called Democracy. The fight would go on, and next time. . . .

Boris Johnson promised himself that at least there *would* be a next time.

*"Order is the enemy of Chaos. But the enemy
of Order is also the enemy of Chaos."*

Gregor Markowitz,
The Theory of Social Entropy

3

The Council Chamber was ostentatious in its simplicity. The walls and ceiling were plain, cream-colored duroplast, and the floor was carpeted by a brown wool rug. The center of the room was occupied by a large, sleekly functional, solid walnut table.

There were four loungechairs on each of the long sides of the table, single loungechairs at the head and foot. In the center of the table sat two unadorned solid silver trays, one holding glasses of various sizes, and the other, as per tradition, three decanters: wine, bourbon and vodka.

From this modest room on Earth, the ten men seated around the table ruled twenty billion people. There was no legislature, no independent judiciary. Every last quantum of power in the Solar System was held by the Hegemonic Council. Five of its members were elected by the Wards (though elections were seldom contested). The other five were chosen scientifically by the System Guardian, the great super-computer which had access to the data banks of all area Guardians.

The Coordinator and the Vice-Coordinator were chosen by that most hallowed of political methods—naked power struggle within the Council.

Vladimir Khustov, the most powerful man in the Hegemony, was speaking in clipped tones of ill-concealed rage: "You find it amusing, do you Jack? And what if it were *you* that they had tried to kill?"

Jack Torrence, the Vice-Coordinator, sipped evenly at a jigger of raw vodka, his thin, rodentlike features puckered into a sardonic grin.

"But Vladimir," he said slowly, "After all it *was* you they were shooting at, not me. Personally, I think the League showed excellent taste."

"We all know how eager you are to become Coordinator," Khustov snapped. "And I know how desolate my death would leave you. But even you should be able to understand that the fact that the League almost killed a *Hegemonic Coordinator* is what counts. What if you were to become Coordinator, Jack? Would you enjoy being shot at?"

Torrence weighed his next words, ran his gaze quickly over Obrina, Kuryakin, Lao, Cordona and Ulanuzov— Khustov's five sure captive votes on the Council—and when he spoke, he was really speaking to them.

"Perhaps it would not be so bad," he said, "if my friends in the Brotherhood of Assassins were there to protect me."

"That remark was totally uncalled for!" Khustov snapped, and his followers looked properly scandalized. But only *properly*, Torrence noted with interest.

"Maybe you'd like to install a Beam and Eye in the Council Chamber, Vladimir?" suggested Torrence. "That would certainly take care of 'uncalled for' remarks." Steiner and Jones, Torrence's men, dutifully chuckled.

"I'm sick of your brand of humor," Khustov said. "This is a serious situation. The Democratic League may be ineffectual, but it's the only real enemy we have, the only obstacle to complete Order. Once the League is eliminated, we'll be able to go on to establish absolute control of the entire human race. Look how far we've come already! Three short centuries ago, the human race was on the verge of destroying itself. The Greater Soviet Union and the Atlantic Union were ready to fly at each other's throats. If the Sino-

Soviet war hadn't brought them to their senses . . . Well, fortunately both sides realized in time that the human race needed *Order* to survive. And now, after three hundred years, look what Order has achieved. Disease all but wiped out. War eliminated. The living standard quadrupled. And I tell this Council that the League is the only real obstacle to even more complete control. Once we are rid of them, we can afford to install Beams and Eyes everywhere. Or why stop there? Why not control genetics as well as environment? I tell you, we are just beginning!"

Torrence sighed. Every time Vladimir spouts off like that, I have a hard time deciding whether he's an utter imbecile, or just a bigger hypocrite than I am, he thought. One would think he really believes that the so-called Guardian executions for Unpermitted Actions are really the omniscience of the computers we pretend they are instead of mere random blowing of Beams!

"And for this millennium to come about," Torrence drawled, refilling his jigger, "we have to spend millions of credits and tens of thousands of man hours rooting out a bunch of hare-brained romantics? Come on, Vladimir, as you said yourself, our control is already all but total. Do we *really* have to treat a tired joke like the League as if it were a serious threat?"

"When was the last time *you* were shot at?" Khustov blurted.

Time to apply the needle! Torrence thought. "Aha!" he said. "Now we come down to it! *You* have been shot at, and *this* is the great threat. This is what transforms a pack of fools into a dangerous conspiracy. Tell me, Vladimir, why aren't you as hot to eliminate the Brotherhood? After all, they've caused far more trouble than the League. Could it be that you know something about the Brotherhood that we don't? Could it be that you and the Brotherhood have . . . *an understanding?* After all, they *did* save your life. . . ."

Torrence noted with considerable satisfaction that even Khustov's men on the Council looked rather thoughtful now.

"You're going too far, Torrence!" Khustov roared. "The

Brotherhood is just a collection of religious fanatics, like the old Judeo-Christians. How do I know why they saved my life? They say the old religionists used to cut open the guts of animals and decide what to do on the basis of how the entrails fell out. The Brotherhood of Assassins is cut from the same cloth. The Judeo-Christians had their Bible, the Communists had their Marxlenin, and the Brotherhood has Markowitz and his *Theory of Social Entropy*. It's all the same kind of meaningless mumbo-jumbo. Religious fanatics may be pests, but they can't be a serious threat because they don't even live in the real world!"

"And the League, of course," Torrence said, "is a perfectly real menace?"

"Yes, it is, because they offer what is superficially a real alternative. What if they *had* killed me?"

Torrence laughed. "Don't ask me to be so crude as to answer *that*," he said. For the millionth time, he wondered how Khustov could keep power—and the answer was the same: five other Councilers believed the same garbage he did. And no wonder, since Obrina, Cordona and Kuryakin had all been selected by the Guardian.

"I mean *aside* from your becoming Coordinator! The League could then boast that they had killed a Coordinator, and over live television to boot. No doubt they had an annunciator bomb all set to go off as soon as I was dead. They were moments from becoming a genuine threat."

"And the Brotherhood of Assassins robbed them of that pleasure," said Torrence. "Most . . . ah . . . *curious.*"

"Damn you, Torrence, I—"

"*Please*, Councilors," Councilor Constantine Gorov said, and Torrence groaned. This bald-headed, emotionless creature was the closest thing to a human computer that Torrence had ever met—a fitting choice indeed by the Guardian for the Council. Gorov was brilliant in an academic way. You had to give him that, Torrence thought. But when it came to dealing with human beings, the man was a tiresome imbecile.

"Don't you see that this is exactly how you're *supposed*

to react to the Brotherhood's actions?" Gorov said earnestly. "If one studies the *Theory of Social Entropy* and the rest of Markowitz' work, it becomes plain that the very randomness of the Brotherhood's activities is a pattern in itself. We are certain, as Vladimir has pointed out, that the Brotherhood believes in the work of Markowitz much as the Judeo-Christians used to—"

"Enough, Gorov, enough!" barked Khustov. "This is getting us nowhere. We must act! I think that it is safe to say that no one on this Council, not even our good Vice-Coordinator, can see any reason why the Democratic League should continue to exist."

"Hardly the point," Torrence said tiredly. "It's the cost that I object to, the cost of ferreting two or three thousand League members out of a population of twenty billion."

"But what if we could break the League's back cheaply?" Khustov said.

"I gather you have a proposal to make," Torrence said. "Please go ahead and make it." This was all becoming pointless, he thought. Vladimir had the votes to push virtually anything through the Council.

"Very well. First of all, we must tighten up security. Guards must be more carefully screened and must be required to undergo depth interrogation every six months. That should eliminate any further League infiltration of the Guards. All in favor?"

The approval was unanimous. Even Torrence could find no reason for not going along.

"Second, the proper professionals in the Ministry of Guardianship should be instructed to evolve a cheap plan for destroying the Democratic League."

Again, the vote was unanimous.

"Finally, I propose that our original schedule for installing Beams and Eyes in all new dwellings be advanced so that such installations shall begin immediately."

Torrence grimaced. To him, the whole matter of Eyes and Beams was ridiculous. To be sure, the Guardians actually could detect and deal with really gross violations of the Code, but the widespread belief that the Beams would kill for even minute violations was just propaganda, propaganda reinforced by killing hundreds of innocent Wards at random. The danger was that Khustov and Gorov and their kind would someday try to turn propaganda into truth— and if control got *that* tight, nothing would ever be able to dislodge Khustov.

But the vote on the proposal was strictly a power struggle, with only Torrence, Jones and Steiner voting against it. As Torrence had expected, Gorov went along with the majority—even though he was just not human enough to be part of Khustov's cabal.

The asteroid's orbit carried it several degrees above the ecliptic, and much closer to Jupiter than the other rocks in the Belt. It was a tiny worldlet, about a mile in diameter, and there were thousands of other asteroids just like it. It was worthless, useless, and far, far off the normal shipping lanes between Mars and the Jovian satellites. By all the logic of economics, logistics and astrogation, it would remain unused forever.

Therefore, it was inhabited.

But the habitation was undetectable from space, for all the installations were underground—in fact, it would be more accurate to think of the asteroid as a building, since chambers and passageways and droptubes honeycombed it completely. Near the core of the asteroid, a nuclear reactor, shielded far more heavily than safety required, provided power—it was important that no detectable radiation leak off into space.

For this was the headquarters of the Brotherhood of Assassins.

Arkady Duntov stood mutely in a great chamber in the bowels of the asteroid, a chamber whose walls and ceiling and floor were the rock of the asteroid itself. He stood facing a massive round table, also carved from the living rock and continuous with the floor. Eight men were seated around the table, dressed in plain green shorts and T-shirts—standard wear for a closed environment—and each man wore a gold medallion on a chain around his neck. The medallions bore the letter "C" raised above a blackened background.

Although the table was perfectly round, one man, it seemed to Duntov, made the place at which he sat the head of the table by his very presence at it. He was old, how old Duntov could not tell, for his long, thin hair was still black and his copper skin had carefully leathered into a neat network of a million tiny wrinkles. His deep black eyes were but vaguely oriental, but his high, blunt cheekbones made his ancestry clear.

"In the name of Chaos," he said, in a surprisingly powerful voice, "I, Robert Ching, First Agent, call this meeting of the Prime Agents of the Brotherhood of Assassins to order."

It seemed to Duntov that nothing could be more purely ceremonial, for he could not imagine these men in a state of disorder. He had been in this chamber five times before, yet still these men were but names to him—Ching, N'gana, Smith, Felipe, Stiner, Nagy, Mustafa, Hoover—the Prime Agents, men so remote, placid, sure, that he was content to follow them without question, without knowing their first names—and without wanting to know.

"We will now hear the report of Agent Arkady Duntov, who was in charge of our recent Martian operation," Robert Ching said. "Proceed, Brother Duntov."

Arkady Duntov took a deep breath. Several of the Prime Agents—Hoover, Felipe, Nagy—might be less than a decade older than himself. Yet he felt as if he were addressing a conclave of ancients.

"Yes, First Agent," he said, his broad, rather Slavic face solemn and half-downcast. "As I was ordered, I left my primary assignment and proceeded to Mars where I met five other Brothers. According to plan, we strolled casually about on the secondlevel street by the Ministry as the Coordinator's speech was about to begin. After the riot started, and the League agent in Khustov's personal bodyguard turned his gun on the Coordinator, we burned him down. We then dispersed and after the search for the League agents had subsided, regrouped at our ship in the desert and I returned here to report."

Although he knew he had carried out his orders to the letter, he had the uneasy feeling that perhaps he had somehow failed, that these men must judge him by standards he could never comprehend.

"So," said Ching. "And what of the League agents? What of Boris Johnson?"

"Nine League agents were captured, First Agent. Johnson was not among them. Since the Hegemony hasn't announced his capture, I would assume that he was able to leave Mars."

"Ah!" exclaimed Ching. "A total victory for Chaos! It is well that Mr. Boris Johnson escaped. Indeed, had he been captured, we might have decided to intervene on his behalf. It is interesting, is it not, how the Democratic League, despite its so-limited resources, still manages to somehow survive. . . ."

"It could very well be merely a run of Random Factors favoring them," suggested the tall, thin African who Duntov knew only as N'gana.

"Perhaps," replied Robert Ching. "But then, it is not merely a run of favorable Random Factors which enables *us* to survive, now is it? Planning is required. For instance, how were Brother Duntov and his men able to wait out the Hegemonic search on Mars while the League agents had to flee or face certain capture? Both groups had perfect papers. The League, however, forges *papers,* while we forge *people.* Six Wards disappear and are replaced by six Brothers, altered, where necessary, to be their exact duplicates. By using real papers and false people, we have no need to fear the Guards checking papers against the records. Planning, Brother N'gana! It is heresy to equate the Reign of Chaos with mere luck."

"Well taken, First Agent," said N'gana. "My point was that the Democratic League does not seem to be terribly long on planning—or on brains, for that matter."

"Do not mistake ignorance for stupidity," said Ching. "After all, the Wards of the Hegemony are kept in total ignorance of the Way of Chaos, of the Law of Social Entropy. And that, of course, includes the Democratic League. It is not their fault that they must grope in the dark, unsure of their way. Rather than laugh at their numerous failures, we should admire them for their few successes, since, though they grope, they grope for the right reasons."

"Their hearts may be pure," N'gana said dryly, "but they are rapidly becoming a Predictable Factor."

Ching frowned, nodded, and said, "Perhaps you are right. But now is not yet the time to make such decisions. We have another report to hear, and this one, I'm sure, will cause nothing but pleasure."

Duntov, who had been listening in growing confusion to the conversation that had been going on almost entirely over his head, took a step toward the door, but Ching called him back. "Brother Duntov," he said. "You have served Chaos well. I deem it fitting that you be allowed to remain."

"Thank you, First Agent," Duntov said dutifully. He wondered if he really wanted to learn more of the cause he served. Wasn't it enough to serve a cause, men, one could believe in, without being expected to comprehend the incomprehensible?

Ching pressed a button on the small communicator-console built into the table. The door opened, and a tiny, whizzened old man entered with energetic little mincing steps.

Murmurs swept the table. "Schneeweiss?" "News of the Project?"

Ching smiled. "I believe that all the Prime Agents know Dr. Schneeweiss, and vice versa. Dr. Schneeweiss, let me introduce Brother Arkady Duntov, a most valuable field agent."

"You . . . you are Dr. *Richard* Schneeweiss?" Duntov stammered. "*The* Schneeweiss? The Hegemony thinks you're dead!"

Schneeweiss laughed sharply. "A gross exaggeration, as you can see," he said. "I am very much alive, and very much at work."

"You've been a Brother all along?"

"No, my boy," Schneeweiss said, "not all along. But as a physicist, my work took me further and further into certain areas which lead towards increased Social Entropy, in the long run. And when Councilor Gorov, a most perceptive man, realized the direction my work was taking, he reported it to the Council, and the Council, somewhat to Gorov's displeasure, discontinued my subsidy. The next step, no doubt, would've been to . . . ah . . . discontinue *me*. It was then that I was approached by one of my assistants, who had been a Brother for years. My 'accident' was arranged, and here I am."

"Come on, Doctor," broke in the one called Smith, whose hard, intense blue eyes were at strange variance with his corpulent body, "you may chat with Brother Duntov at another time. Let's hear the latest about Project Prometheus!"

"Yes, let's have the progress report!"

"Very well, gentlemen," Schneeweiss said. "Let me say that the theoretical work has been completed, the technical details more or less ironed out, and a small model is in the process of being successfully tested right now. Moreover, the preliminary work on Prometheus itself is well under way, and we can expect that Project Prometheus will be operative between four to six months."

"Only another half year!"

"The end of Order is at last in sight!"

Robert Ching laughed mirthlessly, and it seemed to Duntov that his large black eyes were gazing off into some vast and mystic vista which he alone, of all the men in the room, truly saw. "Yes, my Brothers in Chaos," Ching said, "Project Prometheus is no longer a dream; it is fast becoming a reality. For three centuries, we have fought the deadly Order of the Hegemony of Sol, bolstered only by our knowledge of Markowitz' great work. For three hundred years, we have kept our faith in the inevitable triumph of Chaos. And now, the beginning of the end of the Hegemony is come at last. In six months, the work of three centuries will come to fruition, and the unnatural rule of order will begin to crumble, though it may take decades to fall.

"And the Reign of Chaos will at last resume."

Arkady Duntov had the feeling that if he pressed Ching or Schneeweiss, he could learn things that no Ward could even imagine. But somehow, he let himself be dismissed without uttering a word. Some things it was better, perhaps, not to know.

It was enough to follow those who knew them. It was good to follow the Way of Chaos, good to have faith in the triumph of something greater than Man. But it was something else again to try to *understand* the force called Chaos.

"It is a simplistic error to equate Chaos with what is vaguely called the Natural State. Chaos underlies the increasing entropy of the raw universe, to be sure, but it also fills every interstice in that most defiant of anti-entropic constructs—Ordered human society."

Gregor Markowitz,
The Theory of Social Entropy

4

The spires of the tallest buildings in Greater New York soared a mile into the sky, and there were scores of such man-made mountains. There were thousands of buildings—older skyscrapers, newer residences—over seventy stories high, and all these buildings were linked together at numerous levels by glideways and elevated streets and liftubes and droptubes, forming one vast multi-leveled aerial warren that stretched from Albany in the north to Trenton in the south, from Montauk in the east to Paterson in the west, from the clouds above to the original groundlevel below, a level all but indistinguishable from the scores of levels tiered above it.

But having pierced the clouds, having piled level upon level above the ground until the entire city was all but one unthinkably huge building, greater New York, unlike its ancient ancestor, stopped at groundlevel.

And below groundlevel was a vast undergound labyrinth, a forgotten, hidden city of abandoned subway tunnels, sewer mains, trans-Hudson tunnels and tubes, ancient grottos that had existed as far back as the forgotten American Civil War. This abandoned honeycomb beneath the city crossed the Hudson by the moldering Tube Tunnels, by The Holland and Lincoln Tunnels, the Metroway subway tunnel. All but forgotten by the Hegemony, totally forgotten by the Wards, erased from the history and guide books, unpatrolled by the Guards, berift of Eyes and Beams, unmapped and perhaps unmappable, this subterranean labyrinth was the furtive citadel of the Democratic League.

Making his way along the abandoned subway tracks between the old 116th Street and 125th Street stations, the thin brilliant beam of his flash the only light in the all-enveloping velvet darkness, Boris Johnson savored a rare moment of utter security.

The subways were League territory. In fact, this underground city, and similar abandoned man-made grottos beneath Chicago and Bay City and Great London and Paris and Moscow and Leningrad and scores of other multi-leveled cities all over Earth, were all that stood between the Democratic League and extinction. Above was control, Guards, Beams and Eyes, paper checks. But a man could disappear into the underground ruins until the necessary papers were forged when things got too hot up above. Here arms could be cached, meetings held, papers forged, in security. No doubt the Hegemonic Council was aware of the uses to which the abandoned warrens were put, but to seal the myriad forgotten entrances, to install Beams and Eyes in every tunnel under every city, to patrol the tunnels, was clearly impossible. And to blast the tunnels shut would crumble the cities above at their roots, so honeycombed with the abandoned tunnels of centuries was Greater New York and the other huge cities.

The tunnels, like the League, were nuisances too picayune to justify the enormous expense of total elimination, and in that economic calculation lay the League's precarious safety.

Now Johnson reached the 125th Street station. Ahead, he saw a circle of flash beams lighting up the blackness of the station platform—the others had already reached the meeting place. Johnson scrambled up out of the right-of-way cut by a corroded metal ladder and stood on the station platform, amidst rotten remains of wooden benches, decayed vending machines, the cracked and pitted asphalt of the platform itself.

Stumbling over amorphous lumps of rusted metal, great chunks of buckled asphalt, he reached the circle of men that hunkered near the stairs that led upward to groundlevel and the sealed station entrance, covered with parkland, which the League had broken into, then covered again with a great divot of earth and grass, thus becoming one of the scores of hidden accesses to the subterranean maze beneath the gleaming city.

Twelve men hunkered in a circle, their faces illumined only by the light of individual flashes—ten New York Section Leaders, and two others.

Lyman Rhee, a pale, gaunt, ghostly creature who had spent the last five years beneath the city, who had committed the unthinkable crime of killing a Guard in full sight of a crowd of Wards, and who, marked by the bone-white skin and pink eyes of albinoism, could only remain alive here, hidden from view, like a pallid worm, a moleman condemned to perpetual darkness. There were others like Rhee who lived in the subways, but none had lived underground longer, and none, so it was said, knew the maze so thoroughly. Rhee was the Section Leader of the small army of ghosts that haunted the hidden, forgotten bowels of Greater New York.

Johnson smiled as he saw that the twelfth man was indeed Arkady Duntov, his right-hand man, the closest thing he had to a friend. A man so plain and ordinary that he was not even on the Hegemonic Enemy list—and yet a man who always seemed to come up with surprising information and plans, as if he had access to some hidden store of wisdom beyond his own seemingly-modest mental resources. Johnson did not understand the blond, broad-faced Russian, but he valued him as one of the most useful agents the League had.

Heads nodded and greetings were muttered as Johnson stepped within the circle, hunkered down above the cracked, grimed asphalt of the station platform.

"Well I suppose you all know what happened on Mars by now," Johnson said glumly.

"The tv and the fax sheets all say that the Brotherhood

tried to kill Khustov, not us," Luke Forman said, his black face etched to a mask of ebony confusion by the light of his flash. "What happened, Boris?"

Johnson grunted. "What do you think, Luke?" he said. "The Brotherhood actually *saved* Khustov, and then the Council must've decided that it would be better to blame the Brotherhood for the attempt. The Wards think of the Brotherhood as a natural calamity, so it's better for the Hegemony to blame them than to admit that *we* can be dangerous. You know the official line on us—we're a joke, an amusement to be reported with the sports results, if at all. If we had killed Khustov, they would've had to change their tune, but as it is. . . ."

"We're right back where we started from," Mike Feinberg said, grimacing.

"Which is exactly nowhere," Manuel Gomez added. "Membership is decreasing. The Wards are getting fatter and happier every day. More Eyes and Beams everywhere. And we can hardly make anyone aware that we exist. I hate to say this, Boris, but at times like this, I wonder if we're even *right*. No more war, the standard of living going up, everybody happy. . . . Maybe we should break up the League and just try to live with it—get ours while we can. Do we even know what this Democracy we're busting ourselves for really is? Maybe it's just a word. Maybe it doesn't mean anything at all."

"Come on Manny," Johnson said, forcing a tone of certainty into his voice. "We all know what Democracy is. It's . . . it's being able to do what you want, how you want, and when you want to do it. Democracy is everyone doing what's best for himself, not having other people, or the Guardian running every minute of his life."

"If everyone does what he wants," Gomez said, "then what happens when desires conflict?"

"Er . . . the majority rules, of course," Johnson said vaguely. "The majority has to go along for the good of all."

"That doesn't sound a hell of a lot different from the Hegemony."

Johnson frowned. This kind of talk was getting them nowhere. The time to worry about just what Democracy was was after the Hegemony was destroyed and there was leisure to argue about the fruits of victory. And that was a long, long way off. *Action* was what counted now. Too much thinking about ends led only to confusion. . . .

Lyman Rhee expressed Johnson's unvoiced thoughts. "This is not the time to discuss trivia," the albino said shrilly. "For five years, I've rotted in these tunnels, and there are scores like me. Democracy is when we can come out into the sunlight again. That's good enough for me, and it should be good enough for you."

"That's exactly the point," Johnson said. "We're all rotting in one kind of darkness or another. Democracy is light, and we can't expect to see what that light can show us until we have it—and we won't have it until we bring down the Hegemony. Now we've got to plan our next step."

"I don't see where we have much choice," Gomez said. "We don't have the men to start a real revolution, and even if we did, we couldn't get the Wards interested because the Hegemony controls all the media and keeps the Wards fat and happy. Way I see it, all we can do is keep trying to kill Councilors. If we succeed, at least then they'll have to take us seriously, and then maybe some of the Wards will start to think. . . ."

Most of the men nodded in agreement.

"You're right, of course," Johnson said. "The question is, which Councilor, and where and when and how. Gorov? Steiner? Cordona?"

"What does it matter?" Rhee said. "A Councilor is a Councilor."

"Perhaps not," Arkady Duntov said. Johnson studied his broad features, wondering if Duntov was about to come up with something again.

"The man we should kill is Vice-Coordinator Torrence," Duntov said. "Everyone knows he wants to be Coordinator, which makes him Khustov's enemy. If we kill Torrence, *everyone* will start to think. Is the Brotherhood the enemy of the League? Was Torrence aligned with the Brotherhood? If the Brotherhood is supposed to have tried to kill Khustov, and then Khustov's enemy Torrence is killed, the Council can't blame *that* on the Brotherhood! They'll be forced to give us the credit!"

Where does he get it from? Johnson wondered. For Duntov clearly was right. If they could kill Torrence now, Khustov's cleverness in blaming the attempt on his life on the Brotherhood would backfire. He would be forced to blame Torrence's death on the League—or it would be blamed on *him!*

"Isn't Torrence supposed to speak at the Museum of Culture here next week?" Johnson said. "He's the easiest Councilor to get to because he's always making public speeches, trying to undermine Khustov. Now how do we go about. . . ?"

"The Museum is at groundlevel!" Rhee suddenly exclaimed. "Yes! Yes! And there's a subway station right under the auditorium. They'll be guarding Torrence heavily, but they won't think to. . . ."

"Just how close to the auditorium is this station?" Johnson asked.

"There's an old entrance right under it!" Rhee said. "The Museum was built where there used to be a big plaza, above the 59th Street station. There were many exits. They just sealed the exits with plasteel when they razed the plaza and built the Museum right over the old station. The auditorium's right on top of one of the sealed exits. A foot or two of plasteel—that's all we'd have to go through to get into the auditorium."

"I've got a better idea," Johnson said. "We don't even have to get into the auditorium—just put a nice bomb under the floor. Torrence will never know what hit him. We'll meet in the 59th Street station—you, Rhee, of course, and me, and . . . Feinberg, you're our best explosives man, you bring the stuff. We'll—"

"What was that?" Forman suddenly shouted. The shout

echoed down the subway tunnel, echoed and echoed . . . and the echoing did not die away. . . .

And Johnson heard the echo of Forman's shout become the hollow, staccato sound of feet coming toward them from downtown, in the roadbed cut to the left of the platform—many feet, close, and coming closer.

"Kill the lights!" Johnson hissed, extinguishing his own flash and drawing his lasegun. The footfalls came closer in the now-total darkness, their pace seemed to increase.

"At least twenty men," Rhee hissed in Johnson's ear. "In the station now! Listen! Hear how the sound changes as they emerge into the greater volume of the station! Ten . . . thirteen . . . seventeen . . . twenty-two. . . . That's it, twenty-two of them."

"Do you think they've heard us?" Johnson asked.

Rhee laughed softly. "Sound carries for miles here," he whispered. "If we heard them, they heard us."

"Keep your lights out," Johnson ordered. "If they turn theirs on first, they'll be sitting ducks—and vice versa." He searched his mind, tried to remember the layout of the station in the pitch darkness.

"The roadbeds are about six feet below this platform," Rhee said. "If we drop down into the opposite cut so that the platform is between us and those Guards, we'll be hidden from them."

"Okay," Johnson said, easing himself over the lip of the platform and carefully lowering himself down onto the rotten wooden ties and corroded rails that floored the roadbed cut. "Make it quiet. If we sit tight enough, maybe they'll pass us."

Quickly, the League agents slipped over the edge of the station platform and down into the roadbed cut as the footfall sounds came ever closer. . . . Now they seemed to be nearly opposite them, in the roadbed cut at the other side of the platform.

Johnson held his breath, not daring to make the slightest sound. The Guards in the opposite cut made no sounds, other than the sounds of their feet, and kept their flashes dark.

Then Johnson heard soft grunts and the sounds of men pulling themselves up onto the platform. From the platform, he realized, the Guards could use their flashes and see the entire station. But they would have to expose themselves to do it. . . .

Johnson tightened his grip on his lasegun.

Suddenly the platform before him was bathed in light. His eyes struggled to adjust for a moment; then he saw five Guards carrying flashes in one hand and laseguns in the other standing above him on the platform, not ten feet away.

Before Johnson could give an order, Forman and Gomez and several others he could not make out opened up with their laseguns. Cruel lances of intense red light speared the Guards on the platform. They screamed, blackened, collapsed in smoking heaps. Their flashes, still on, fell every which way, striping the darkness with crazily intersecting beams of light, dotting the gray tunnel walls with bright yellow circles.

But the Guards still down in the cut had spotted them. Using the platform between themselves and the League agents as cover, they began firing their laseguns over the heads of the League agents.

Johnson ducked down below the lip of the platform as a lasebeam seared the air inches from his head. By the deadly red flashes of the lasebeams tracing patterns of fiery death above their heads, Johnson could see all his men crouching low on the roadbed. They were pinned down. The Guards were pinned down too—Johnson lifted the barrel of his lasegun over the lip of the platform and got off a quick blind shot—but the Guards could expect reinforcements.

"We've got to get out of here. . . ." Johnson muttered.

"Listen!" Rhee said beside him. "More Guards coming up from the south, lots of 'em!" Over the hiss of the laseguns, Johnson could sense a faint, far-off rumble, a rumble that was felt more than heard, approaching like a pressure-wave up the tunnel.

"We've got to split up!" he said. "Half of you head south, rest of you come north with me. As soon as you come to a branch tunnel, split up again. They can't follow all of us. Don't try for an exit until you're sure you've lost 'em."

Johnson led Duntov, Rhee, Forman and two others he could barely make out in the laser-lit semidarkness north up the roadbed cut, crouching low to escape the lasegun fire. As they ran along the old roadbed, stumbling over ties, he heard the Guards shouting behind them, men climbing over the platform, then the sound of running feet directly behind them.

"Faster! Faster!" he shouted breathlessly as he ran. "We've got to get to the next station before they catch up!"

They ran through the cut, out of the station, and into the narrower, now-all-but-pitch-black tunnel, tripping over tracks, ties, switches. Behind, they heard the inexorable footfalls of the pursuing Guards, saw the way before them by the dim light of their far-away torches.

About two hundred yards up the tunnel, Rhee whispered, "Junction! Left tunnel is the old express tunnel, goes right to the 145th Street station. Right tunnel passes the 135th Street station. Let's split up here. If we're lucky, they'll only follow one group."

Rhee took Johnson's hand, led him into the deeper darkness of the righthand tunnel. The moleman's hand felt moist and unpleasant in his, and Johnson grabbed someone else's hand, dragged him along behind himself and Rhee. The others took the lefthand tunnel.

He heard the hiss of laseguns behind him as they dashed further up the tunnel, then screams, more hisses. The Guards were fighting with the other group. Did that mean. . . ?

No! He heard footfalls behind him, coming closer. And circles of light from the Guards' flashes danced over the walls of the tunnel not too far behind them. The Guards had split up too!

Lungs aching, Johnson forced himself to run harder as Rhee half-dragged him and the man behind puffed and panted.

Suddenly, Rhee came to an abrupt halt.

"What the—"?

"Listen," the albino said. "Ahead of us! More of them, heading south right for us. We're trapped!"

"Maybe we can fight our way past the ones in front," the third man suggested, and from the sound of his voice, Johnson knew that it was Arkady Duntov.

"There's at least a dozen of 'em," Rhee said. "Can't you hear?" He tittered nervously. "But of course you can't! We're finished—no, wait! There should be one nearby. . . ."

He pulled Johnson along in the darkness, and Johnson dragged Duntov behind him. Rhee seemed to be feeling along the wall with his free hand as he ran. . . .

And then, there before them was a square of gray, a tiny patch of wan light in the pitch darkness.

"Ventilating duct," Rhee said. "Comes up in the ground-level street. If we're lucky and there's no one around up there, we should be able to get out. Take a look."

Johnson stepped into the square of light. A shaft about two feet square angled up at about 45 degrees toward the street. Johnson pulled himself up into the shaft, scrambled up the slime-coated concrete, using his elbows and knees to wedge him firmly against the slippery walls. About eight feet up the shaft ended in an ancient, corroded iron grill. Holding his place in the shaft by spread-eagling his legs behind him, Johnson poked away the amorphous filth around the grill and looked through.

They were in luck! The grill opened beneath the curb of a groundlevel alley behind some apparently abandoned old wreck of a building.

"Hurry up!" Rhee called from below. "They're getting closer!"

Johnson inched back a foot or so in the shaft, took out his lasegun and hurriedly burned through the cornerbolts holding the grill in place. He pushed the hot crosswork of metal outward with the back of his hand, scorching his knuckles in the process.

Quickly, he pulled himself upward, crawled out into the gutter, got to his feet in the wan sunlight, filtering downward through the many levels of glideways, ramps and streets above groundlevel. Duntov emerged, blinking, a moment later, behind him.

Then Rhee's head popped through the hole, a pale, bone-white ghost's head with oriental features and pink rat's eyes. Rhee blinked in the shadowy sunlight, scrunched nearly translucent lids over his eyes.

"I can't see up here anymore!" the albino whined. "Too bright! Too bright!" He brought two scrawny arms up over the lip of the grill opening, held himself wedged in place, kept his eyes tightly shut.

"Come on! Come on!" Johnson urged.

"I . . . I can't," Rhee said. "You go ahead. I'll stay in the shaft until they pass." He laughed bitterly. "I've been down here so long I can't stand the light. But don't worry about me. They'll never catch me in my tunnels! I'll meet you under the Museum as planned."

"Are you sure . . . ?"

"Don't worry," Rhee said. "I'll be there."

Johnson shrugged, nodded to Duntov, and they brushed themselves off, stepped out of the alley onto a nearly deserted groundlevel street.

Johnson glanced once behind him as Duntov, without looking at him, headed away from him up the street into a small knot of Wards.

Rhee was clinging to the lip of the grill opening, just a white head and scrawny nearly bonelike arms visible, eyes tightly shut, a cave thing impaled in the light.

"Paradox is the equation of Chaos."

Gregor Markowitz,
Chaos and Culture

5

"And so, after leaving Johnson and realizing the important nature of the situation, I immediately called for a ship on the secure Brotherhood frequency and reported directly to you, Prime Agents," Arkady Duntov concluded.

Duntov studied the faces of the eight Prime Agents seated around the massive rock table. Almost doglike, he had expected them to be pleased with him—after all, wouldn't the death of Torrence create confusion, increase Chaos? Wouldn't the fact that the Vice-Coordinator could be killed by the League introduce what they called a Random Factor?

But seven of the men before which he stood were frowning heavy, portentious frowns. Only Robert Ching, the First Agent himself, was smiling his thin, enigmatic smile, and what ordinary man could read what *that* meant?

"This plan to kill Torrence, Brother Duntov," N'gana finally said, breaking the oppressive moment of silence, "it was *your* idea, not Johnson's?"

"Yes, sir," Duntov said uneasily.

"Then may I ask *why* you volunteered this scheme?" N'gana said sharply.

"Why are you badgering the boy?" the olive-skinned, natty-featured Brother called Felipe said. "You know his mission as well as any of us—to report on the League and to keep himself in a position to influence the actions of Johnson when we so desire. To do that, it is necessary that he make himself invaluable to Johnson. Therefore, it was perfectly within the scope of his orders to volunteer a plan."

"My point is," N'gana said, "that from our point of view, it's a very bad plan. Why should we want Torrence dead? Torrence is the chief opposition to Khustov on the Council, hence he represents a source of Random Factors. Hence, his death would *increase* Order and *decrease* social Entropy. And that is certainly not what Brother Duntov has been assigned to the League to do!"

"Bah!" Brother Felipe said. "You're too simplistic in your thinking, N'gana. Remember what the Council knows—that we saved Khustov. If we permit the League to kill Khustov's enemy Torrence, it will look as if we're on Khustov's side. *That* will really increase Chaos. It will make every other Councilor wonder about Khustov."

"Perhaps," N'gana conceded. "Nevertheless, the death of Torrence still would remove a source of Random Factors from the Council, even if it would introduce a new one. The real question is, do we gain more than we lose by his death? Is the total quantity of Social Entropy increased?"

Duntov listened to the argument in rapt admiration, amazed at the subtle implications the Prime Agents had discovered in what to him had been such a simple idea. The workings of the minds of the Prime Agents seemed to take place in a dimension far removed from that in which his own brain operated. To him, the Chaos he served was a simple matter—the sowing of confusion, fear and doubt in the enemy camp. But as he listened to the Prime Agents, it seemed to him that to these men Chaos was a living thing, a thing which commanded them as they commanded him. As he was but an instrument of the Prime Agents, so it seemed that the Prime Agents were instruments of something else, something great, superhuman, invincible. And the mystery, the incomprehensibility of this thing called Chaos only increased his dedication to its service. It made him feel he was on the side of something far greater than mere men, something so awesome that in the long run it could never fail.

"Perhaps the most chaotic move," the tall, blond Brother called Steiner observed, "would be for us to kill Torrence ourselves. That would be a truly Random act. It would put Khustov in an impossible position. It would make it appear certain that he was in league with us. The Council would rebel against him, perhaps even have him executed, and without Torrence on the Council, there would be true Chaos, since there would then be no new center around which the power of the Council could cohere."

"But that would make us appear predictable," N'gana said. "It's too obvious."

"On the contrary, it would—"

Robert Ching, Duntov saw, had been listening to all this without so much as changing his unreadable expression, without even looking at the Prime Agents, as if contemplating something even these men could not see. Now he spoke, softly, quietly, and the others instantly fell silent.

"Brother Duntov's plan," Ching said, "has interesting paradoxical implications." He smiled at Duntov. "The very fact that it has occasioned such dispute within our own ranks indicates to me that Brother Duntov has not committed an error. Paradox and Chaos, after all, are very close indeed. Chaos is paradoxical and Paradox is Chaotic. After all, even Markowitz' simplest statement of the Law of Social Entropy is paradoxical itself: 'In social orders, as in the physical realm, the innate tendency is towards increased entropy or disorder. Therefore, the more Ordered a society, the more Social Energy is required to maintain that Order, the more Order needed to generate that Social Energy, the two paradoxical needs feeding upon each other in an ever-increasing exponential spiral. Therefore, a highly Ordered society must grow ever more Ordered, and thus can tolerate less and less Random Factors as the cycle progresses.' "

"Thus," said Ching, "the inevitablity of Chaos. Increasing Order leads as inexorably to Chaos as decreasing Order does. All is Paradox."

Duntov's mind reeled. He had somehow never gotten around to reading the works of Markowitz, though he had heard this standard summation of the Law of Social Entropy before. But he had never thought of it as a paradox. His indoctrination had told him that it meant that any act which disrupted Order served Chaos. It had never occurred to him that Order, Chaos' opposite, could serve Chaos as well. He still did not really grasp the concept, but the very invincible inscrutability of it all filled him with a strange ecstasy. Did the old Judeochristians feel this way about that which they had called "God"? There was something vastly reassuring in the thought that some great superforce underlied all, a force that could be used but never understood. How could the Hegemony successfully combat Chaos when the very act of combating Chaos served Chaos itself?

"I don't see why you're repeating something we all know, First Agent," Felipe said, but with a quiet respect, as if he knew that Ching must have *some* reason, if only because Ching was Ching.

"Because," said Robert Ching, "we do well to remember that we work within Paradoxes which work within other Paradoxes. Obviously, a living Torrence is a source of Random Factors within the Council. Just as obviously, a Brotherhood assassination of Torrence would *also* produce Random Factors, since at the very least it would cast suspicion on Khustov. A fine Paradox—the death of Torrence would increase Social Entropy in one way, but a living Torrence is a source of increased Social Entropy in another. This is the Paradox inside of which we must act."

"It seems to me," N'gana said, "that we must simply choose that course which will maximize Chaos. Our most basic strategy is to introduce Random Factors into the closed system of the Hegemony—at least until Project Prometheus is completed—and within a Paradox like this, we must choose the best of two compromise courses. We can't have it both ways."

"Ah, but why *not* have it both ways?" Robert Ching said. "We keep Torrence alive, and the conflict between him and Khustov generates Random Factors. But what if we were to kill Torrence? Better yet, what if both the Brotherhood and the League were to kill Torrence? First we frustrate the League by saving Khustov from them, then we seem to be allied with them, and with Khustov as well when we both try to kill Torrence. True Randomness!"

"You've lost me now, First Agent," N'gana said. "How can we kill Torrence and keep him alive at the same time?"

"We do not have to *succeed*, do we?" Robert Ching said. "It is only necessary that we *seem* to try to kill Torrence. With a live Torrence convinced that we tried to kill him while we saved Khustov—you see the possibilities? Moreover, if we can save Torrence from the League by attempting to kill him. . . ."

Slow smiles inched across the faces of the Prime Agents. Apparently, Duntov thought, they understand what he's getting at. I wish I did. . . . Or do I? Perhaps there are some things it is better not to know. . . .

Boris Johnson climbed up onto the platform of the abandoned 59th Street subway station, saw by the light of his flash that Mike Feinberg had already arrived.

He made his way to the center of the platform, where Feinberg stood, holding two metal cannisters, a big brush, and a small metal box.

"Rhee hasn't gotten here yet?" Johnson asked.

"I haven't seen him," Feinberg replied. "I've got the stuff here, but we can't do anything without Rhee. I can't find my way around this place. There are lots of exits up above and the whole upper roof is a sheet of plasteel. Who knows which exit the auditorium is under? You don't think the Guards could've caught Rhee?"

"Not down here!" Johnson said. "Rhee's hardly human anymore. He can see down here, but he can't see in the light. But if something *has* happened to him—"

"Don't worry about me!" a sibilant voice suddenly hissed behind him.

Johnson whirled in time to see the pale figure of Lyman

Rhee dart out from behind a cracked pillar. The man moves like a ghost! he thought.

"I wish you wouldn't do that," Johnson said. "Sneaking up on people's likely to get you killed."

Rhee laughed shrilly. "It's become a habit that's hard to break," he said. "But come, let us go about our business."

Rhee led them up a flight of crumbling asphalt stairs to a large low-ceilinged chamber that had been the upper level of the station. The ceiling, low as it had been in the ancient days, was even lower now, for a thick layer of plasteel, shiny and out of place in the ruins, had replaced the old concrete ceiling of the chamber, and it was atop this strong base that the Museum of Culture had been built.

The albino led them to a barricade of old, rusted turnstiles which sealed off the rest of the station from the exits. They climbed over the corroded turnstiles, were led by Rhee past a concrete box that seemed to Johnson to be some kind of sentrypost. Then Rhee led them up a short flight of stairs which ended abruptly, sealed off in mid-flight by the plasteel foundation of the Museum which was a good deal lower than the old roof of the station.

Rhee placed his ear against the plasteel ceiling which cut across the stairwell and listened silently for a few moments.

"Yes!" he finally said. "This is the one. We're right under the auditorium now, in fact right under the podium itself. Listen! The place is beginning to fill up. I can hear the vibrations of many feet, except directly above us, which means that the stage has to be here. We're in luck, and we're on time!"

Once again, Johnson marveled at the keenness of the albino's ears, and his certain knowledge of the subterranean world. The Hegemony had created for itself a formidable enemy indeed when it chased Rhee to these grottos.

"Okay," Johnson said. "Let's get to work."

Feinberg opened one of his cannisters. He dipped his brush into the viscous gray stuff inside, began spreading it on the plasteel ceiling which sealed the subway exit.

"This is a nitroplastic," he said, as he brushed the stuff on the ceiling. "Very powerful, and it dries almost instantly."

After a few minutes' work, the entire area of plasteel bounded by the concrete mouth of the stairwell, about six by nine feet, was covered with nitroplastic. Feinberg put down the brush and cannister, ran his finger across the dark gray coating.

"Good and dry," he said. "Hand me the timer, will you Boris?"

Johnson handed him the small metal box. It had a dial on one face, with an exposed and moveable metal hand, and two sharp metal prongs on the opposite face.

Feinberg jammed the timer against the nitroplastic. The prongs stuck in the coating, held the timer to the ceiling.

"The stuff is electrically detonated," Feinberg said. "I can set the timer for anything up to an hour. How long do you want me to set it for?"

Johnson thought for a moment. Torrence was scheduled to begin speaking in a few minutes. He might babble on for an hour or so. The timer should be set for a delay just long enough to give them time to get safely away. . . .

"Give us half an hour," he told Feinberg.

"Right," Feinberg said, positioning the pointer on the timer's dial. "Now for the reflector. Hand me the other cannister and the brush, will you."

Feinberg began smearing a gummy white paste over the layer of nitroplastic. "Interesting stuff," he said as he worked, carefully covering every square inch of the dried nitroplastic with the paste. "Explosive reflector. I don't know exactly how it works, but what it does is reflect back all the downward energy of the nitroplastic at the moment of explosion. It forces all the power of the blast upward, right under Torrence. You could stand right under here when it goes off and not be hurt—except for falling chunks of plasteel, of course—but up above. . . . They'll have to scrape what's left of Torrence off the auditorium ceiling!"

Feinberg finished his work, shined his flash on it. Every

inch of nitroplastic, and even the timer box, was covered with the white paste.

"Okay," he said. "All set. We've got twenty-five minutes to get out of here. Then—goodby, Jack Torrence!"

Johnson grinned smugly as they quickly descended the stairs. Not even the Brotherhood could save Torrence now! There was no way to stop the explosion—even if someone knew the stuff was there. And nobody outside the League did!

Jack Torrence entered the big auditorium of the Museum of Culture through the entrance at the rear behind a screen of Guards and counting the house as he made his way down the center aisle towards the small stage with its plain podium. He noted with some slight satisfaction that though the hall was only about half full, all the Wards that were there had been crowded into the front half of the auditorium, as per his instructions, so that the television cameras at the rear could shoot zoom shots of him over their heads as he spoke, thus creating the illusion of a packed house.

And of course, Torrence thought, it's what the tv screens show that really counts. The Wards were stupid sheep—if you showed 'em how popular you were often enough, they'd believe that you *were* popular, and if they thought you were popular, they'd jump on the bandwagon and really make you popular.

Popularity itself did not matter to Torrence. But the fact was that a Councilor's term was ten years, and several would expire soon. If he could build himself up as a figure greater than the Council, as Khustov had, he might be able to elect one or two more of his flunkies to the Council. If he were popular enough, it might even affect the Guardian's choice of Councilors, since internal harmony on the Council was supposed to be one of the computer's criteria in choosing its five Councilors. It's never too early to campaign, he thought. Especially if Vladimir really has the Brotherhood in his hip pocket.

But that really wasn't likely. Vladimir's right about the Brotherhood, he thought, they're just religion freaks. *But*, hinting at collusion is a good weapon to use on Vladimir now and then. Gorov's a swing man, more machine than the Guardian itself. If his vote ever should really count, tying Vladimir to the Brotherhood just might bring him over. . . .

Torrence mounted the low stage, stood behind the podium and rustled the papers before him. Today's speech was to be about the beneficent effect of Order on Art, which to Torrence meant the effect of bushwah on baloney. The truth was that there was hardly anything to make speeches about at all. You could only praise the peace and prosperity so often. The Wards would not be exactly overjoyed to hear that Eyes and Beams were to be installed in all dwellings, and it was against policy, and for good reason, for one Councilor to publicly criticize others. It was also against policy to rail against the League or the Brotherhood—no point in giving publicity to either. So you spoke about trivia, like Art. The Wards didn't care what you said anyway. All that counted was showing your face.

Torrence glanced at the television crew. The director gave him the high sign. He was on the air.

"Wards of the Hegemony," he began, "it is fitting that we are gathered today in the Museum of Culture, for Art and Culture are the highest achievements of any civilization, and the Hegemony of Sol is the highest civilization the human race could hope to achieve. We sometimes forget that in the mad Millennium of Religions, Art, as well as Man, was at the mercy of hundreds of conflicting dogmas and theories. It is difficult for us today to realize that the Art of that black period was torn every which way by the aesthetic precepts of every hare-brained cult or social misfit who—"

Suddenly, there was a commotion at the rear of the auditorium. Torrence saw the rear door glow red, then fall abruptly inward. Two men carrying laseguns stood in the doorway. Torrence ran his finger across his throat, signaling the television crew to stop transmission, then dived for cover behind the podium as Guards sprang up before the stage to protect him.

"Gas!" someone shouted, and the Wards began screaming and howling. Torrence looked up over the edge of the podium, saw a cloud of thick green vapor all but obscuring the rear of the auditorium. He recognized the gas as Nervoline, a contact-toxin whose very touch was instant death. . . .

In the front of the auditorium, Wards were leaping up out of their seats, screaming in terror, milling about mindlessly. The gas reached the television crew, and the men fell, silently, instantly, dead before they hit the floor.

Torrence felt a long moment of utter mortal panic as the gas crept toward the front of the auditorium. The only exit was cut off by the green vapor itself.

But Torrence' moment of terror passed as he realized that whoever had thrown the gas grenade had aimed badly, very badly indeed. The gas cloud was too small to fill the auditorium and now it was rapidly dissolving. Nervoline was a riot control gas which the Guards used as a screen behind which to advance, and thus its toxic effects had to dissipate rapidly. The stuff did not linger long in the air. To be effective, the grenade should've hit near the podium, but it hadn't. Someone had made a mistake—or perhaps had been forced to throw the grenade without taking proper aim by the Guards in the building.

Torrence stood up. The gas was all but gone. The television crew was dead, but he was safe, and the Wards were beginning to calm down. Torrence laughed, half to relieve the tension, half in real amusement.

It was a piece of typical League bungling, he thought. They couldn't even—

Suddenly, he saw a small metal ovoid whirring above the heads of the wards. Half-involuntarily, he ducked down behind the podium again, then almost as quickly stood up as he realized that the thing was only an annunciator bomb.

"Death to the Hegemonic Council!" a loud, tinny voice boomed. "Long live Chaos! Know that Vice-Coordinator Jack Torrence has been destroyed by the Brotherhood of Assassins!"

"The Brotherhood!" Torrence exclaimed. "Not the League . . . ?"

He gestured hurriedly to the Guards. "Clear the hall!" he ordered. "You can never tell what the Brotherhood will do. Let's get out of here!"

Torrence stepped down from the stage, and Guards formed a circle around him, quickly ushered him out of the auditorium and into the hall outside.

Torrence, still within the circle of armed men, moved about twenty feet down the hall, turned to watch as dazed Wards began to stream out of the auditorium.

He stood there watching until the hall was cleared. There's something mighty fishy going on! he thought. First the Brotherhood saves Vladimir, then they try to kill me. Maybe I was wrong after all—maybe Vladimir really *has* made some kind of a deal with the Brotherhood. Fortunately, the crazy fanatics seem to be as incompetent as Johnson's boobs.

Still, something will have to be done about this. Maybe . . . hmm, yes, whether Vladimir really is in cahoots with the Brotherhood or not, I certainly can use this against him.

Why not? It's good circumstantial evidence. Maybe I can at least convince Gorov, bring him into my camp. That'd make it six to four, and a one-man switch would tie up the Council and force a general election. Maybe. . . .

"The auditorium is all cleared now, sir," the Captain of Jack Torrence's personal bodyguard said. "Shall I—"

"BAARRROOM!"

There was a terrible, sharp, explosive roar from within the auditorium, then almost at once another loud noise as the ceiling collapsed. A great foul billow of smoke and airborne debris puffed from the shattered doorway. The building shook. Torrence was blown off his feet, and the hefty Guards around him staggered for purchase.

Dazedly, Torrence got to his feet, stumbled over to the doorway of the auditorium, stuck his head inside. Eyes smarting from the smoke, Torrence saw that where the stage he had been standing on had been, there was now only a gaping, jagged hole. The ceiling above the hole had given way, and he could see through the ruined ceiling to the corridor above.

Rubbing his eyes, Torrence withdrew his head from the auditorium. It just doesn't make sense! he thought. A bomb, and right after the Brotherhood just tried to gas me. Why would. . . ?

Unless . . . unless. . . . Unless the *bomb* was planted by the League! Two assassination attempts within minutes of each other! Yes that had to be it. Both attempts couldn't have been part of the same Brotherhood plot. They would've known that if the gas failed, the auditorium would be immediately cleared, that a bomb as a backup device would be useless.

Despite his two close calls, Jack Torrence could not help giving vent to a short, dry laugh. The Brotherhood, by its bumbling attempt to gas him, had actually saved his life! If it hadn't been for the gas attack, he would've been on the stage when the bomb went off and been plastered all over what was left of the ceiling. . . .

Torrence grimaced. That didn't make the whole thing any less infuriating. The League isn't such a harmless nuisance after all, he thought. Vladimir's right about one thing, anyway—the League has to be destroyed, and quickly. Damn the expense! They may very well try something like this again!

But afterward, Torrence thought, after we've dealt with the Democratic League, then we'll get rid of the Brotherhood.

And Vladimir'll have to go along. If he doesn't, it'll be proof positive that he's allied with the Brotherhood, and even his own tame Councilors'll turn on him. Even if he *is* allied with the Brotherhood, he'll have to go along.

And once we've gotten rid of the League and the Brotherhood, Torrence thought resolutely, it'll be time to deal with Mr. Vladimir Khustov himself!

"It is wise, upon occasion, to introduce true randomness into your actions when opposing an existing order. The problem is that randomness, by definition, cannot be planned. Human emotion, however, is a Random Factor, and thus it may be said that to serve the interests of one's own endocrine system is to serve Chaos."

Gregor Markowitz,
The Theory of Social Entropy

6

Foolish, foolish, utterly foolish! Constantine Gorov thought as Jack Torrence continued to rant, ostensibly at Khustov, but of course actually for the benefit of the entire Hegemonic Council.

". . . and I'm beginning to wonder why you're so interested in getting rid of the League, Vladimir," Torrence was saying, his thin face flushed with a rage that Gorov was sure was put on, "while you seem to regard the Brotherhood of Assassins as merely a nuisance to be tolerated. Or *do* you consider the Brotherhood a nuisance?"

Khustov scowled—more ridiculous histrionics, Gorov thought. "What is that remark supposed to mean?" the Hegemonic Coordinator said thickly. Torrence paused, looked each Councilor individually in the eye before he spoke again. As the Vice-Coordinator met Gorov's eyes, Gorov had a pretty good idea of what he was trying to do. All this nonsensical political bickering! One would almost think that the Hegemonic Council existed merely to provide a political arena for fools like Torrence and Khustov rather than as a human adjunct of the Guardian with a solemn duty to maximize Order and insure peace and prosperity for the human race!

"I'm not sure exactly what it means myself," Torrence finally said. "All I'm sure of is the facts—let the Council draw its own conclusions. Fact—the Democratic League tried to kill you, Vladimir, and the Brotherhood saved you, so, perhaps understandably, you are determined to destroy the League, but are somewhat more . . . *sympathetic* to the Brotherhood. Fact—it is an open secret that the two of us are . . . ah . . . shall we say, rivals, in a gentlemanly way, of course. Fact—the Brotherhood, which recently saved your life, has just tried to kill *me*. But who am I to draw conclusions? This Council is composed of reasonably intelligent adults. I think they are capable of drawing their own conclusions."

"I've had enough of your snide insinuations, Torrence!" Khustov roared. Then, colder, "I remind you that the Democratic League tried to kill us both. The League is the primary menace. I remind you that the Brotherhood of Assassins is a cabal of religious fanatics. Who knows why they do what they do?" He stared straight at Torrence, smiled a thin, menacing smile. "And I might further remind you, Mr. Torrence," Khustov said, "that whether you like it or not, I am still Hegemonic Coordinator. To falsely accuse me of treason may be construed as an act of treason in itself. You had better weigh your words more carefully."

"Treason against *who*, Vladimir?" Torrence said. "Treason against *what*? Against the Hegemony? Against the Guardian? Against this Council? Or simply against Vladimir Khustov? Or perhaps against the Brotherhood of—"

"You go too far!" Khustov shouted, his face reddening in now totally genuine rage.

Constantine Gorov could contain himself no longer. The fools were acting exactly as the Brotherhood wanted them to!

"Councilors, please!" Gorov said. "Don't you see what's happening? *This* is why the Brotherhood saved your life, Councilor Khustov! *This* is why it then tried to kill Councilor Torrence. . . . If it really did try in earnest."

"What are you babbling about this time, Gorov?" Khustov snapped. "More of that rot about the Theory of Social

Entropy? One would think you're a member of the Brotherhood of Assassins yourself! Sometimes I wonder if you don't really believe Markowitz' mystical claptrap about the 'inevitability of Chaos.' "

"To rationally oppose religious fanatics," Gorov said evenly, "one must understand the dogma which they serve. Otherwise, their actions become totally unpredictable."

"And I suppose *you* can predict the actions of the Brotherhood?" Torrence sneered.

"To a point," Gorov said, blandly ignoring the sarcasm. "The Theory of Social Entropy postulates that an Ordered Society such as the Hegemony can tolerate fewer and fewer random factors as its control becomes more and more complete. So the strategy of the Brotherhood is obviously to introduce such random factors. In other words, one may predict that their actions will be calculated to be unpredictable."

"Meaningless dialectical gobbledegook!" Councilor Ulanuzov shouted.

Such blind, willfully ignorant fools! Gorov thought. "Not at all," he said evenly. "This present business is a perfect example of Brotherhood logic—or rather, its purposeful lack of logic. By appearing to side with the Coordinator against Councilor Torrence, they foment strife on this very Council. And the both of you are playing right into the Brotherhood's hand. Can't you see that—"

"Enough of this idiocy!" Khustov shouted.

"Enough! Enough!" several other Councilors shouted in agreement.

"For once, I find myself in agreement with our good Coordinator," Torrence said. "This nit-picking and theoretical bull-throwing is getting us nowhere. The real question is, will you finally place as high a priority on the destruction of the Brotherhood as you do on the elimination of the League, Vladimir?"

"The Brotherhood must not be destroyed until the League is eliminated," Khustov said flatly.

"I suppose you can give us some logical reason. . . ?" Torrence said dubiously.

"If you could think of anything beyond furthering your own selfish ends, you'd see what the reason is," Khustov said. "It's obvious—as long as the League exists, the Brotherhood is useful to us. Everything the League does can be blamed on the Brotherhood. The Wards can understand why the League does what it does—they're out to overthrow the Hegemony, pure and simple. But the Brotherhood's ends— if they really *do* have ends—are totally incomprehensible. To the Wards, the Brotherhood is nothing but a pack of religious madmen. It's far safer to blame League assassination attempts and sabotage on madmen than to admit that a coherent revolutionary conspiracy exists and is dangerous. As long as the League exists, the Brotherhood serves us as a convenient, innocuous scapegoat—every act against the Hegemony can be branded as the work of madmen. Once we eliminate the League, I promise you we will give top priority to the destruction of the Brotherhood. But not until then."

"And just when is this millennium going to come about?" Torrence said. "We can control the League, but how can we crush it, short of spending billions of credits? The leadership can always hide in the underground tunnels. There are only a few thousand members and only a couple of hundred key men, but they're scattered all over the Hegemony. Aren't you really saying that we're *never* going to move against the Brotherhood?"

Khustov smiled complacently. "Quite the contrary," he said. "We will soon eliminate the League. We will cause the League to commit its entire leadership to one mission, a mission that will be sure to attract the personal attention of Boris Johnson himself. Once we capture or destroy the leadership, the League will swiftly collapse."

Gorov was bemused by Khustov's apparent certainty. "How do you plan to accomplish this?" he said.

"The Ministry of Guardianship and the System Guardian itself have been working on the problem," Khustov said.

"We have uncovered a League agent in a critical position in the Ministry of Guardianship on Mercury."

"He has been taken alive?" Councilor Cordona asked.

"He has not been taken at all," Khustov replied. "He's far more useful to us where he is. We're after far bigger game. The Hegemonic Council will meet on Mercury two months from now."

"What?" Torrence shouted. *"Mercury?* We've never met on Mercury. There's just one small dome, the smallest and newest in the Hegemony. . . . Why the colony's hardly viable! The Wards don't like being that close to the sun—and neither do I."

"And that will be our cover mission," Khustov said. "We'll announce that the Council is meeting on Mercury in order to demonstrate our confidence in the safety of the dome."

"I don't like it," Torrence said. "It's too confined, too precarious. If the League could concentrate its forces there, they might just be able to kill us all."

"Precisely," Khustov said. "That's exactly what Boris Johnson will think—and all the more so, since he has a key man in the Ministry building where we will be waiting. We'll let him try, and then—the end of the Democratic League, once and for all!"

"You're saying that you intend to use *us* as bait!" Torrence exclaimed.

Shocked murmurs swept the Council chamber. Constantine Gorov, however, was intrigued. What better bait than the Hegemonic Council? he thought. The League would be certain to rise to such a bait. An excellent tactic, he was forced to admit—provided, of course, that the trap was foolproof.

"Gentlemen!" Khustov said, and the Council quieted. "I assure you that there will be no risk involved. This trap will be foolproof." He smiled. "Once you know the plan, I'm sure that even our good Vice-Coordinator will agree."

The Councilors, Torrence in particular, grunted skeptically, but once Khustov had outlined the plan, the vote to adopt it was unanimous. Even Torrence went along with little more than *pro forma* grumbling.

Boris Johnson felt along the wall of the tunnel of the old 4th Street subway station. His fingers found a crack in the concrete almost imperceptibly deeper than any one of a hundred such cracks in the tunnel wall. He pushed the fingers of his right hand into the crack and pulled. A section of the concrete swung inward on hidden hinges, exposing a dark, narrow passageway. Johnson entered the earthen-walled tunnel, pushed the panel shut behind him. Shining his flash before him, he inched his way down the tunnel.

The secret tunnel, cut by the League two years ago, led to the most secure meeting place in the entire Greater New York subway and grotto network—a small, incredibly ancient grotto under what had been MacDougal Street in Old Greenwich Village. The League had discovered it quite by accident three years ago, and not even the oldest maps showed it. League historical experts, such as they were, surmised that it had been hollowed out to hide runaway slaves, long before the American Civil War. It was doubly secure—no one outside the League knew it existed, and even if the Guards searched the 4th Street station, they would not be likely to find the entrance to the passageway cut to the grotto.

Getting to this place is impossible, Johnson thought, but it's worth it. It's worth taking all possible precautions now. At last we have a chance to destroy the entire Hegemonic Council. We'll have to risk everything, but it'll advance our cause by years.

Perhaps . . . perhaps, he dared to think, with the entire Council killed at one stroke, the Hegemony itself may even disintegrate.

At last, he reached the end of the narrow tunnel. The tunnel opened into a hemicylindrical chamber, about seven feet tall at its high point, perhaps ten feet long. The rounded wall-ceiling was mold-encrusted red brown brick and the floor was damp wet earth. It was dank in the grotto, but it was quite warm, for the chamber's temperature was raised considerably by the body heat of the twenty men jammed into the close quarters—all the Section Leaders that could be summoned on short notice, Arkady Duntov of course, and Andy Mason, head of the League Forgery Bureau as well.

"I hope you've got us all stuffed into this hole for a good reason, Boris," Mason, a squat, hawk-featured man said. "It's hotter than hell in here."

"Best reason in the world," Johnson said. "Great news! We're gonna assassinate the entire Hegemonic Council, all at once!"

Made testy by the heat and close quarters, the men muttered half-mutinously. "That's crazy!" Manuel Gomez said. "You dragged us here to tell us that? It's impossible!"

"Haven't you seen any television lately?" Johnson said. "Don't you read the fax sheets? The Hegemonic Council is meeting on Mercury two months from now. It's supposed to prove that the planet is safe or something. But we'll make it mighty unsafe for them!"

"Sure we know about that," Gomez said. "So what? Every planet has a secure Council Chamber in its Ministry of Guardianship building, and you can bet they'll be surrounded by Guards every moment they're outside the Ministry. We'd never be able to get to them outside."

"Right," Johnson said. "They'll be expecting us to try something when they make the trip through the dome to the Ministry, and we wouldn't have a chance then because they'll be ready for us."

He paused. "That's why we're going to kill them while they're inside the Ministry," he said.

"Impossible!"

"Insanity!"

"Not a chance!"

"Have you completely lost your mind, Boris?" Arkady Duntov said. "Every corridor, every room, every nook and cranny in a Ministry building has an Eye and a Beam. You can't even *look* suspicious inside a Ministry. The first move we made, Beam-plugs would pop all over the place. Even if we wanted to try some kind of suicide charge, we wouldn't get ten yards. It's totally impossible."

"That's exactly what the Council would think," Johnson said. "That's why my plan will work." Well, I expected a reaction like this, he thought. It's a good sign. If even my own men think I've gone nuts, the Council should be taken totally by surprise.

"What plan?" Gomez said. "What plan could you possibly have that would let us kill the Council in a building where every room and corridor is equipped with Beams and Eyes?"

"Correction," Johnson said. "There are two rooms in the Ministry that *don't* have Beams and Eyes."

"Oh . . . ?" said Arkady Duntov.

"Sure. The Council Chamber itself, for one. The Hegemonic Council doesn't want the Guardian monitoring their own doings. You can bet that Unpermitted Acts go on in there."

"So what good does that do us?" Mike Feinberg said. "We'd have to get inside the Council Chamber, and that's plain impossible. You know what the security setup is on those Chambers? They're completely surrounded, all four sides, top and bottom, by corridors that are always kept clear. The moment anyone, even a Guard, steps inside one of those corridors without prior authorization, *all* the corridors are immediately filled with radiation. Sure, if we were careful—and lucky—we might be able to get agents into the building, but the moment anyone entered that box of corridors, every Beam in them would pop."

"And what happens to the Council when the corridors are filled with radiation?" Johnson asked rhetorically.

"Don't be silly, Boris!" Feinberg said. "The whole Council Chamber is lined with two feet of lead. They just sit tight till the emergency's over. They're totally self-contained in there."

"And what do they breathe when they're all sealed up in there," Johnson said, "vacuum?"

He could feel the tension suddenly rise in the dank grotto as the men suddenly fell utterly, raptly silent.

"It's typical of the Hegemony," Johnson said. "Everything's supersecure. And *there* is the weak point! A diversionary attack on the outside of the building should make them seal off the Council Chamber, right? No sweat there. So once the Council Chamber is sealed off, where do they get their air supply from?"

No one ventured a guess.

"We've got an agent inside the Mercury Ministry of Guardianship, in Maintenance," Johnson said. "As soon as I heard about the Council meeting on Mercury, I got a full plan of the building from him. When the Council Chamber is sealed off, air is supplied by lead lines from a small pumproom two floors below. We don't have to get into the Chamber. Once the Chamber is sealed off, all we have to do is drop a vial of nerve gas concentrate into the air lines at the pumproom end."

"But how can we do that?" Feinberg said. "The moment we get into the pumproom, the Beams'll pop."

"Think, man, think!" Johnson exclaimed excitedly. "How could there possibly be Beams in the pumproom? Remember, in an emergency, the Council is completely dependent on the pumproom for air. They wouldn't *dare* have Beams in there—because if they did, anything—a wrong word, a false move—would kill the men in the pumproom with radiation. If that happened at the same time that the Chamber was sealed off, the Councilors would suffocate. No, all they have in the pumproom itself is about half a dozen Guards guarding the Maintenance personnel. And of course the door and walls of the pumproom are lead-lined in case something makes the Beams in the adjacent corridors pop. If we can get half a dozen men inside, we can gun down the Guards, close the lead door, and gas the Councilors through the air lines before anyone can possibly break in."

"But how do we get inside the pumproom?" Gomez said. "The moment we start burning through the door, the Beams in the outside corridor will pop."

"You're the expert, Feinberg," Johnson said. "How much delay between the time an Eye spots an Unpermitted Act and the time the corresponding Beam pops?"

"Two, three seconds at the very most," Feinberg said.

"And how long before the radiation in the immediate area reaches a lethal level after a Beam pops?"

"Say, another two seconds maybe."

"Well," said Johnson, "that gives us five seconds from the time we make our move to get inside and get that lead door shut behind us."

"It just can't be done," Feinberg said. "We can't burn our way in that fast with laseguns, or even blast our way in that quick. Come to think of it, we can't do either, since we'll have to have that door intact to seal the room off when the Beams pop."

"Right," Johnson said. "But what if the door is opened for us? Six men could jump inside and get the door shut behind them in five seconds, couldn't they?"

"Of course," Feinberg said. "But what are we going to do, knock on the door and ask the Guards to let us in? The Guardian might even consider *that* an Unpermitted Act."

"That's the easiest part of all," Johnson said. "What worries me, is can we forge enough travel passes to get a couple of hundred agents to Mercury in time for the festivities? What about it, Mason, can do?"

"It won't be easy," Mason said, "but it can be done. But just how do you intend to get into the pumproom?"

Johnson laughed. "That agent I mentioned," he said, "the one on the Ministry Maintenance staff? Name's Jeremy Daid—and he works in the pumproom."

Johnson grinned broadly, as the mood of the men abruptly changed, as they nodded their heads, smiled at him. They were confident now, as he was. It all sounded so terribly improbable until that final revelation—and then, it was all so obvious.

Still, it was hard to get used to, hard to get used to the fact that after ten years of failure at far less ambitious projects, the Democratic League was so close to destroying the entire Hegemonic Council. And there wasn't a flaw in the plan that Johnson could see. . . .

Arkady Duntov paused, stared nervously around the rock-walled chamber, studied the stolid, calm, unreadable faces of the eight Prime Agents of the Brotherhood of Assassins. Seven of them seemed lost in thought, as if still weighing the new information. But Robert Ching seemed to be smiling knowingly. But what could the First Agent know that the others didn't? Or *was* it a matter of knowledge? Perhaps Ching knew no more facts than the others, perhaps it was his very mind that was different, a mind that saw relationships where others saw only chaos—and a mind that saw Chaos where others saw Order?

"So Johnson plans to assassinate the Council by gassing them through the air lines," Duntov continued. "The League agent in the pumproom will let them in. They'll probably pay with their lives for their success—the plan seems to have no provisions for escape, but . . . Boris does not usually think that far ahead, and perhaps, even if he has, he's probably willing to make the sacrifice."

"What do you make of it, First Agent?" Brother Felipe said.

"Yes, First Agent, what do you think?"

The Prime Agents watched Robert Ching, waiting for him to speak. But when Ching spoke, he turned to Duntov, standing before the massive rock table, smiled blandly and fixed Duntov with a mild yet penetrating stare that made him somehow nervous and reassured at the same time.

"What do *you* think, Brother Duntov?" Ching asked. "You were there, you know Boris Johnson."

"What . . . what do I think about *what,* sir?" Duntov stammered.

"About Johnson's plan, to begin with," Robert Ching said.

Duntov himself wondered what he really thought of Johnson's plan. He began to muse aloud. "Well, it's quite complicated, to be sure. . . . By attacking the Ministry from the outside, they get the Council to seal the Chamber. . . that should work. If they're very careful, and lucky, they should be able to get half a dozen agents to the pumproom door at the right time without arousing suspicion. Not an easy thing to do, but the League has had plenty of practice in that kind of thing. . . . And once inside the pumproom, they'd have surprise on their side and they should have no trouble eliminating the Guards—and then killing the Council will be child's play. Obviously, the key factor is getting inside the pumproom within five seconds of the time the Beams in the corridor pop. *If* they can do that, the plan should work. And they *do* have an agent in the pumproom. . . ."

"So . . ." said Robert Ching, "an excellent analysis, Brother Duntov. You see what this implies, do you not, Brothers?"

Duntov saw that the Prime Agents were staring at Ching blankly, as ignorant of that which was obvious to Ching as he himself was.

Robert Ching seemed to sense this, and he laughed. "Consider," he said. "The Hegemonic Council's lives are at stake. The Democratic League is risking its very existence. Hundreds of men involved. . . . Either the death of the entire Hegemonic Council in the event of success, or the destruction of the Democratic League in the event of failure. And all this, the entire plan, hundreds of lives, depends on one man. *One man!*"

Suddenly, Duntov saw it, and now of course it was obvious. It all came down to Jeremy Daid, the man in the pumproom!

"The League agent in the pumproom. . . ." he muttered.

"Exactly," said Robert Ching. "Consider . . . *if* this Daid succeeds in getting Johnson and his men into the pumproom, the Hegemonic Council is doomed. If he fails, the Council survives and the Democratic League is doomed. One man . . . what does this suggest to you, Brothers?"

"The Hand of Chaos!" Smith exclaimed. "Perfect Randomness! That the fates of both the Council, with its rigid Order and great resources, and the Democratic League, with its complicated planning, should be determined by one man, who is himself a mere pawn! Chaos, sheer Chaos!"

Robert Ching smiled. "I think not," he said. "Consider. Consider the Hegemony, so tightly Ordered, with such complete, near paranoid security arrangements. Does it not seem peculiar that the Hegemonic Council should happen to be meeting on the one planet where the League happens to have an agent in the one place that will enable them to assassinate the Council? Does it not seem strange that the Hegemony, with its Guardians and its Guards and its psychoprobing and its obsession with security should not have discovered a League agent in such a sensitive position? When so many Random Factors seem to correlate, one should begin to suspect the Randomness of it all; one should begin to see the hand of Order operating behind the facade of seeming Chaos. . . ."

"What are you getting at, First Agent?" Brother Felipe said.

"Consider," said Ching. "What more irresistible bait for the Democratic League than the entire Council? A bait so irresistible that it would seem like a trap even to the naive Mr. Johnson—were it not for the secret advantage he fancies himself to have in the agent in the pumproom. But *whose* edge is Mr. Jeremy Daid? The League's—*if* the Council is ignorant of his connection with the League. But if the Council is aware of what Jeremy Daid is, and is using him as part of the bait. . . ."

"Of course!" Duntov blurted. "The whole thing's a trap!"

Ching nodded. "I think we can safely assume that it is," he said. "Though of course we have no way of knowing just what the details of the trap are. But that need not be a factor—we can assume that the Council's plan, whatever it is, will work. In matters such as these, Mr. Boris Johnson is no match for Vladimir Khustov. The question before us, is what action do *we* take?"

"Perhaps we should take no action at all," N'gana suggested. "Though the League is superficially the enemy of the Hegemony, if you analyze its actions in terms of the social dynamics of the Theory of Social Entropy, you realize that far from being a true Random Factor, far from increasing Social Entropy, it is actually a predictable factor—the "Disloyal Opposition"—and thus it *decreases* Social Entropy. Why not let the Hegemony destroy the League? We should welcome its destruction—especially with Project Prometheus so far advanced."

"You have a point," Robert Ching said. "Yes . . . the League must be eliminated soon, and now is as good a time as any. But I don't think it should come about as the result of a successful trap set by the Hegemony. That would increase Order. Besides, while I do wish to see the Democratic League removed as a Social Factor, I don't want to see Boris Johnson killed."

"You're going soft, First Agent," N'gana chided. "I do believe you've developed a certain fondness for Johnson!"

Ching smiled, "Why not?" he said. "I admit it. The man is a bumbler, he stumbles in the dark, ignorant of even the Democracy he professes to champion. He does not even have the assurance of the Theory of Social Entropy that the Hegemony must someday collapse. The history of the Democratic League is a catalogue of dismal failure. Yet still he fights on. Blind courage is, after all, a Random Factor. So is heroism. So too, for that matter, is sheer stupidity—and Johnson, paradoxically, is a source of all three. Besides, the man is on the same side as we are, when all is said and done. We both fight for the same goal—the destruction of the Hegemony and the freedom of Man. Despite his many shortcomings, does not such a man deserve better than death at the hands of the Hegemony?"

Brother Felipe laughed. "I do believe that all your logic is merely a rationalization for emotion, First Agent," he said, not unkindly. "You allude to Markowitz simply to justify your emotional desire to save Boris Johnson!"

Robert Ching smiled, then shrugged. "Again, I plead guilty," he said. "But consider: is not emotion itself a Random Factor? If we save Boris Johnson for no rational reason whatever, are we not remaining true to Chaos? Observe: I do not suggest we save the League, only Johnson. The League must be destroyed, yet not by the Hegemony. We must interpose ourselves between the Council and the League. First we save the League from the Council, in such a way that it is clear that *we* are doing it. Perhaps . . . yes, we should have both the League and the Council at our mercy. Then we pick and choose. Who is saved and who is destroyed should be our prerogative. And . . . yes, there is a way we can destroy by saving!"

"I gather you are hatching a plan of your own, First Agent," Felipe said.

"Indeed!" said Robert Ching. "And this will be the most purely Chaotic thing we have ever done. Markowitz would be most amused. In fact, short of an Ultimate Chaotic Act, nothing we could do could be more Chaotic."

Arkady Duntov glanced around the table. The Prime Agents were nodding in solemn agreement though they knew not what the plan was. They agreed because Ching was Ching. And Duntov, even knowing that he was more ignorant than the rest, found himself agreeing too, agreeing with what he knew not. . . .

Now Ching turned to Duntov. "I think the time has come for you to sever your relationship with the Democratic League, Brother Duntov," he said. "In fact, I think it only fitting that you lead our little expedition to Mercury yourself. You have served Chaos secretly, Arkady Duntov, and you have served Chaos well. It is time you looked a bit closer upon the face of that which you serve. It is time you served Chaos directly. I have plans for you, Brother Duntov, plans as big . . . as big as the Galaxy."

Duntov was struck dumb. He could only nod woodenly. He felt exalted, exalted by something he could not understand, something he served on blind faith, something he suspected he would always serve out of faith alone. Now his faith was to be rewarded, somehow.

Yet the thought was bittersweet. For faith was what he had lived by, faith in a great unknown. Would that faith be lessened by closer contact with men who were closer to Chaos than he could ever be? Or would it be strengthened?

*"If a man asks you, where can this Chaos of
which you speak be detected by human senses,
take him outside at night and point to the
stars—for in the limitless heavens themselves,
shines the countenance of Chaos."*

Gregor Markowitz,
Chaos and Culture

7 ————————————————————

This far southwest, many miles beyond what had once been
Newark, the periphery of Greater New York was a seemingly
endless expanse of huge, low, glass-roofed buildings—mile
upon mile of hydroponic greenhouses, completely covering
the Jersey lowlands like an immense, glaring mirror.

Only the center express strip of the glideway that crossed
the glass plain, arrow straight on elevated pylons, was occupied, and that but sparsely. For the only thing at the end
of this particular glideway was the city spaceport, and interplanetary travel was rigidly controlled by the pass system,
and as such, systematically discouraged.

Boris Johnson stood on the express strip of the glideway,
squinting against the flashes of sunlight reflected like passing
floodlight beams in his face as the glideway whisked him
towards the spaceport at thirty-five miles an hour. His lug-
gage had already been tubed to the spaceport ahead of him,
but the three most important items were secreted on his
person.

A vial of nerve gas concentrate was concealed in the
hollow heel of his left shoe. A lasegun, disassembled, was
hidden all over him—parts of it sewn into seams of his clothing, other parts in his other shoeheel, still others brazenly
tucked in his underpants.

But neither the gun nor the vial of gas would ever be used unless at least two of the three sets of forged identity papers he carried passed inspection by the Guards.

Johnson had been living in Greater New York under the name of "Michael Olinsky," a television technician, a low-status identity that would not attract undue attention—a standard League practice.

But "Olinsky" could have no reason for traveling to Mercury that the Guards or the Guardian would accept. Therefore, Mason's forgery factory had produced a new set of papers for "Daniel Lovarin," representative of United Techtronics, with a travel pass to Mercury, ostensibly for the purpose of sizing up the prospects for building a factory on Mercury to produce office computers. A good front it was, since the Hegemony was most anxious to attract industry to the still somewhat questionable Mercurian environment dome.

Once on Mercury, "Lovarin" would disappear, and Johnson would become "Yuri Smith," maintenance worker in the Ministry of Guardianship. If the assassination succeeded, and if he were able to escape, he would return to Earth on papers made out for "Harrison Ortega," a Mercurian adman on his way to Earth to organize a campaign to bring more Wards to Mercury—another reason for travel that would be highly approved by the Hegemony.

Johnson grinned as he patted the "Lovarin" papers in his breast pocket. It was hard, sometimes, to keep identities straight, to remember who you were supposed to be at any given paper check. But constant changes of false identities were essential. "Lovarin" had a right to travel to Mercury, "Smith" had a right to be in the Ministry, "Ortega" would have a right to go to Earth. But if any one "man" had papers that entitled him to all three, it would certainly seem highly suspicious. Ordinarily, the Guards simply scanned papers themselves, to see if the description and the photo on them matched that of the bearer. Sometimes they spot-checked retina patterns against the patterns on the papers. The papers would easily pass any such inspection. But if anything seemed out of the ordinary, the Guards would cross-check the papers with the memory banks of the Guardian, and then they would learn that the papers were forgeries—that the "man" they were made out for did not in fact exist. So, many sets of ordinary papers were far safer than one set with too many passes attached.

Ahead on the horizon, the glare of the greenhouses faded away, and Johnson saw that he was rapidly approaching the large, open, concrete field and low terminal building of the spaceport. Soon he would either be on his way to Mercury, or . . . or he would be dead.

But there really didn't seem to be too much chance of that. Everything had gone much smoother than he had really expected. The Democratic League had never tried to move more than a few dozen agents between planets before; now they had to get two hundred men to Mercury within two months. The forgery section had worked day and night to produce the necessary papers in time. Johnson had coldly calculated that a dozen or so agents would be caught in transit—by the law of averages, the Guards would've figured to check at least some of the false papers with the Guardian. As long as only a few agents were caught, suspicion would not be aroused. Johnson had expected to lose a few men in transit and had planned accordingly.

But so far, surprisingly, better than a hundred and fifty League agents had left Earth for Mercury, and not one had been caught. They were the cream of the crop, too—everyone wanted in on this one, and Johnson had felt that he owed it to the leadership of the League to give the assignment to those who had earned it by service. It was a fantastic run of luck that none of these men, many of whom were very high on the Hegemonic Enemy list, had been caught. Well, he thought, the League has had such bad luck ever since it was founded, that it was about time fate evened things out!

Now the terminal building loomed just ahead, and Johnson stepped outward onto a decelerating strip, then outward again to a slower one, and again and again, and he was standing on the concrete apron in front of the building.

He could see the blueish alloy hull of a big passenger ship standing tall and sleek just the other side of the white plasteel terminal building. Not many ships lifted from this civilian spaceport on any given day, and in fact, the ship just beyond the building seemed to be the only one in port at the moment—so it had to be the Mercury liner.

Johnson trotted up the broad, short flight of synthstone steps that led to the wide, doorless portal of the terminal building, and stepped inside under the watchful eyes of four big, brutal-looking Guards who stood, two-by-two, flanking the entranceway.

The interior of the building was one huge lobby, with a series of ten portals along the wall facing the main entrance, numbered in order by illuminated signs. Only one of the signs—number seven—was lit, meaning, as he had surmised, that flight seven, the Mercury flight, was the only scheduled lift-off of the day. He nervously noted that the other three walls of the big room were studded at regular ten-foot intervals with Eyes and Beams.

Johnson took his "Lovarin" papers from his breast pocket, and stepped quickly through the portal marked "seven." He found himself in the familiar lumipanel-lit Coupletube. The flexible Coupletubes were permanently connected to the terminal portals at one end, while the other end was connected directly to the airlock of a loading ship. The Coupletubes were yet another security device, for where a short line of Wards had queued up at the far end of the tube immediately in front of the airlock, four Guards stood athwart the Coupletube going over papers and occasionally checking retina patterns against the papers with the small Eyebox one of them held. And this was the only possible entrance to the ship.

Johnson joined the line, recognized Igor Mallionov, one of the League agents assigned to the Mercury mission two slots ahead of him. They both carefully avoided even glances of recognition.

A burly blond Guard scanned Mallionov's papers then waved him into the airlock. The Ward in front of Johnson showed his papers, was cleared, and then it was Johnson's turn.

Although he had passed such checks with forged papers more times than he could remember, Johnson could not help tensing up as the big Guard held out a pawlike hand and grunted "Papers!" So much more than his own life depended on every move he made from here on in. . . .

Silently, Johnson handed the Guard the "Daniel Lovarin" papers with the attached travel pass.

The blond Guard glanced perfunctorily over the papers, looked up once at Johnson as he checked the photo on the papers with Johnson's face.

He was about to wave Johnson on, when the Guard holding the Eyebox said, "Let's check this one's papers."

The blond Guard shrugged, unclipped a small piece of film from Johnson's papers, handed it to the other Guard. The other raised the Eyebox. It was a small metal box, with a red light and a green light on top, on either side of a slot that fitted the piece of film. There was a button on the rear of the Eyebox and two eyepieces in front.

The thing, Johnson knew, was a standard security device. The retina film was dropped in the slot, the subject's eyes placed against the eyepieces. When the button was pressed, a microcamera in the box viewed the retinas and overlayed the live retina patterns on the ones on the film. If they matched, the green light went on—all clear. If they didn't, the red light flashed—the man didn't match his papers: an Unpermitted Act punishable by death.

The Guard dropped the retina-film into the slot, wordlessly held the Eyebox up to Johnson's face—every Ward in the Hegemony was all too familiar with the procedure. Johnson stared into the darkness behind the eyepieces.

He was momentarily blinded by a brilliant flash of light as the Guard pressed the button and the Eyebox compared the retina film with the illumined backs of his eyeballs.

Then the Guard lowered the box and waved Johnson ahead into the ship, handing him his papers.

Johnson rubbed his eyes and heaved a sigh of relief as

he stepped into the airlock—even though he had known that the patterns would match, the fear-reflex was deeply ingrained.

Another Guard ushered him into a lifttube whose antigravs wafted him smoothly upward and deposited him in a large cabin where perhaps half of the hundred and eighty Gee-Cocoons were occupied.

Johnson picked a Cocoon—an open metal half egg—and sat down on the padded couch inside. The eliptical rim of the Cocoon reached up almost to his neckline.

After about ten minutes, and after perhaps another dozen Wards had entered the cabin, a klaxon sounded.

Hundreds of tiny pores in the metal of the Gee-Cocoon extruded fine plastic filaments. In a few moments, the stuff completely filled the Cocoon, enveloping Johnson's body so that only his head, resting on the headrest of the couch, was free. He was swathed in the stress-absorbent packing like a fragile piece of glassware cushioned in excelsior.

Then the ship's antigravs cut in, and he felt a moment of weightlessness as the ship and its contents were screened from the Earth's gravity.

It lasted only a moment, for then the ship's thrusters came on, and although he and the ship now had no weight, they did have inertia. He was pressed down into the Cocoon as the ship lifted, protected from the force of the thrust by the soft, stress-absorbing packing.

Johnson felt a great spasm of exhilaration as he was pressed down against the couch. Home free! Nothing could keep him from reaching Mercury now. Stage one of the plan was successfully completed!

Robert Ching studied the bland, calm faces of the seven Prime Agents of the Brotherhood of Assassins seated around the great rock table and thought of how different their calmness was from that of Arkady Duntov who stood before him.

What to make of men like this Duntov? Ching thought. Ignorant, but blissful in his ignorance. A man of action and nothing else, yet at the same time submissive to the orders of anyone to whom he could feel inferior, *wanting* someone to feel inferior to. Why does such a man submit to Chaos rather than to the Hegemony?

"The ship is ready to depart, Brother Duntov?" Ching asked.

"Yes, First Agent."

"You understand your orders?"

"Yes, First Agent."

"You have no further questions?"

"No, First Agent."

Robert Ching sighed. What indeed to make of an Arkady Duntov? A man who rebelled against Order, yet always sought something else to obey, something greater than his own soul. A type that persisted, the dogmatic religionist, in an age when there were no longer any religions. Yet to a Duntov, who sought but to worship and not to comprehend, was not the Brotherhood a religious organization, would not Chaos appear as a god? Certainly the Brotherhood attracted enough of these simplistic religious types at the lower levels. Yes, no doubt to the Duntovs, Chaos was a god, and the service of Chaos a religious calling. Or perhaps more precisely, the need for religion persisted in such men and they were attracted to the Brotherhood because Chaos was the closest thing to a god that there was. . . .

What was it that Markowitz had written about god and Chaos? "God is the mask men erect facing them to hide from the unacceptable fact of the Reign of Chaos. . . . God is that which fearful men must postulate, the omnipotent ruler of a superhuman Order, in order to protect themselves from the awful truth that the seeming randomness of the universe is *not* an illusion caused by the inability of mortal Man to completely comprehend the all-encompassing Order of God, but that Chaos itself is the ultimate reality, that the universe, in the last analysis, is based on nothing more structured or less indifferent to Man than Random Chance. . . ."

What irony, Ching thought, that men who search for a god to believe in should be drawn to the service of Chaos, the blind random truth behind the desperately Ordered illusion of a tidy, god-ruled universe! What irony—and yet, what a perfectly Chaotic situation!

"Very well, then," Ching said. "You will now join your men on the ship and leave for Mercury immediately."

"At once, First Agent!" Duntov said. He turned smartly on his heels and left.

Watching Duntov go, Ching wondered whether perhaps the Duntovs did not possess a kernel of the truth. Perhaps, in a way, the Brotherhood *was* a religious order. Did a religion need an anthropomorphic god? Or merely the certain knowledge that there was something bigger than Man and his works, something that would always, in the end, frustrate the absolute, certain Order that Man was forever trying to imprison himself in? Did it matter that that omnipotent something was not a god, was not any being, but the ultimate tendency inherent in everything in the universe, from atom to Galaxy, toward ever-increasing entropy, Chaos itself? Perhaps, in its own way, Chaos *was* a god-immortal, infinite, omnipotent. . . .

"It goes well, eh First Agent," Brother Felipe said, breaking into Ching's reverie. "This Duntov is not very complex, but he is good at following orders, and—"

"It's back! It's back!"

Dr. Richard Schneeweiss suddenly burst into the chamber, his little arms waving wildly, his tiny, almost elfin face flushed with excitement. "It's back! It's back!" he shouted.

"What's back?" several of the Prime Agents said in unison as Schneeweiss stood, arms akimbo, by the table.

"The probe! The probe!" Schneeweiss exclaimed. "The Prometheus Probe. The interstellar instrument package! It's returned from the 61 Cygnus system. The faster-than-light drive is a success. The film is being processed in the photo lab right now."

A bubbling wave of excitement swept through the room. Even Robert Ching bolted to his feet, grinning like a boy. At last! he thought. The first stage of Project Prometheus is a success! The drive works! And now the probe has returned with pictures of the first extra-Solar planet human eyes have ever seen. . . . Ching knew that this was a great moment in scientific history, but to him it was more, so much more. It was no less than the beginning of the end of the Hegemony, the prelude to the ultimate triumph of Chaos. And what, he thought, will the film show? A habitable planet beyond the Solar System, beyond the control of the Hegemony? Perhaps even. . . .

"Come on!" Schneeweiss shouted. "Let's get to the projection room. They should have the edited film ready to roll by the time we get there."

"Indeed," said Ching, "let us see this with our own eyes."

He led the Prime Agents and Schneeweiss out of the chamber and into a corridor hewn from the rock of the asteroid, down the corridor to a droptube, which lowered them gently further down into the labyrinthine catacombs which permeated the asteroid.

As the antigravs lowered him down the droptube, thousands of questions flitted through Ching's mind. Did 61 Cygnus have a habitable planet. . . ? How many? Might not there be . . . another intelligent race working out its destiny around that distant sun. . . ?

They reached the bottom of the droptube, hurried down another rock-walled corridor, reached a small auditorium where a screen was set up before several rows of seats. At the rear of the auditorium, a technician had set up a projector.

As Ching and the other Prime Agents took seats near the screen, Schneeweiss held a quick, hushed conversation with the projector technician, which Ching could not make out. The physicist's face became wild, ecstatic, and Ching had to suppress an impulse to demand an immediate report— but no, this was something to experience through one's own senses!

"What you will see is of course an edited summary of what the probe cameras saw, greatly speeded up," Schneeweiss said. "But nevertheless, you will see. . . . Ah, but I should not tell you, you must see with your own eyes! Let us have the film."

The screen came alive, and Ching saw a great spangle of stars against a black background. As he watched, the film seemed to jerk many times in succession, and one of the stars began to grow in fits and jerks, dominated the others, became a visible disc, which grew and grew. . . .

"The approach to the 61 Cygnus system," Schneeweiss' voice said from the back of the room. "A system of five planets. . . ."

The image on the screen abruptly changed, and showed a jagged barren rock careening through velvet black space. . . .

"The outermost planet, dead, airless, about the size of Luna," Schneeweiss said.

Images of two great banded planets flickered on and off the screen in rapid, staccato succession—the first red, orange and yellow, the second banded with blues and blue-greens.

"Two gas giants, roughly the sizes of Uranus and Saturn respectively," Schneeweiss said. "One tiny inner planet, two-thirds the diameter of Titan."

The screen showed a small black disc, cruelly outlined in the blazing light of the nearby star.

"*And* . . ." Schneeweiss said, pausing dramatically, "the second planet! 1.09 Earth diameter, oxygen-nitrogen atmosphere, .94 standard gravities! In the liquid water zone! Look!"

A blue-green disc appeared on the screen, grew in rapid jerks of perspective to the size of an orange, a melon, a great sphere that all but filled the screen. Ching gasped as he saw great oceans, four brown and green continents, ice caps at both poles, winding rivers, islands, cloud masses. . . .

The camera perspective jumped again, and now the screen showed an aerial view of a large section of one continent— green, obviously wooded areas, rivers, blue lakes: life! The camera-angle narrowed, the area shown was smaller, the details clearer: woods, grassy rolling plains, and . . . and cultivated fields! There was no mistaking the bands of vegetation—orderly rows and checkerboards on the plains, sinuous bands following the contours of the hills—for anything else!

"Yes!" said Schneeweiss. "Sentinent beings, undoubtedly! But there's more! Look!"

Now the camera seemed to be diving towards the surface, in great jumps of increased magnification and narrowing field of vision. The camera seemed to hang for a moment over a stretch of coast where a large river emptied into the sea. . . . And then the view jumped again, and the screen showed. . . .

A city! Scores of square miles of tall, silver buildings, along both banks of the river, lining the seacoast. Long docks reached fingers out into the river. Roads led out into the surrounding countryside. Tiny flashes of light seemed to be flitting about above the city like mites. . . .

Then suddenly, the camera angle changed wildly, as if the probe had violently rolled. Blue sky, fleecy white clouds filled the screen, and then. . . .

A shiny, red, metallic ovoid suddenly filled the screen. The front end seemed to be somehow translucent, there was a ring of ports or nozzles or lenses girding its middle, and a short coil of some blue metal at the rear end. . . .

Then the screen went blank.

"Do you all realize what this means?" Ching exclaimed.

"Of course!" said Schneeweiss. "An alien civilization, and a very high one too! The most—"

"Much more than that!" Ching said. "Consider: we've just discovered sentinent beings in the first solar system we've investigated, a close neighbor of ours, in Galactic terms. Don't you see what this implies? It means that the Galaxy must swarm with intelligent races, hundreds, thousands, perhaps millions of them! Chaos, Brothers, Ultimate Chaos! A vast Chaotic concourse of civilizations, millions of them and each one unique. Random Factors beyond counting! The true face of Chaos—an infinite universe with an infinity of civilizations, no two alike!"

"Chaos!" "Chaos indeed!" "The end of the Hegemony!" "The final defeat of Order!" Everyone was shouting at once. "Yes," said Robert Ching, "and—"

Suddenly a shrill, jarring siren-sound filled the room. *The alarm!* Something was approaching the asteroid. Has the Hegemony at last discovered this base? Ching wondered.

"The alarm!" N'gana shouted. "Of all the times to be discovered by the Hegemony!"

"Quickly!" Ching shouted. "To the observation room!"

They rushed from the auditorium and down the corridor as the siren continued its warning wail, and into another droptube which lowered them down to the very core of the asteroid near the heavily shielded reactor room.

The droptube seemed to end in empty space itself. Ching and the others floated out at the bottom of the tube into a black, gravityless void; they were surrounded on all sides, top and bottom, by the black of space and the piebald jewels that were the stars. Only the opening of the droptube itself, a weird "hole in space" above them, betrayed the fact that they were really still in the asteroid, that the black, starfilled space in which they seemed to float was but an illusion, an illusion created by the great globular viewscreen in which they floated, at the gravityless core of the asteroid, like embryoes in some huge transparent egg.

Illusion or not, Robert Ching felt an exhilarating, oceanic vertigo as he floated in "space" scanning the image of the stars all around him for the intruder, whatever it was. He always felt close to Truth here, close to Chaos. Many were the hours he spent alone in the observation room, contemplating the infinity of the universe, feeling it, seeing it all around him, a vast ocean of primal Chaos before which Man was dwarfed, and, being dwarfed, transfigured. . . .

But this, the still-wailing siren reminded Ching, was no time for contemplation. "What is it?" he said into seemingly-empty space. "Have you fixed its trajectory yet?"

From speakers behind the viewscreen panels, a voice sounded as if from the stars themselves: "Unknown located, First Agent."

A red circle appeared around a point of light in the black pseudo-space. Ching now saw that the point of reddish light he had taken for a star was actually waxing, forming a disc, rapidly approaching the asteroid. But . . . but not from sunward, from the direction of Earth! It was coming from *outward*, from the direction of Saturn or Jupiter. If the Hegemony were searching for the Brotherhood headquarters, the ship should almost certainly be coming from sunward, not from the Outer Satellites. . . .

"Where is it coming from?" Ching said.

"We're not sure, First Agent," the disembodied voice said. "From Plutoward, in general, but we've backtracked its path clear beyond Pluto's orbit, and it intersects no planet or moon. It . . . it seems to be coming from nowhere—unless it's been taking evasive action—or from . . . *from interstellar space*. . . ."

Ching stared at the others floating beside him, stared particularly at Schneeweiss. The physicist was in turn staring at the object approaching the asteroid, which now showed an unmistakable disc; which was so close that the disc could be seen to grow, second by second.

How big is it? Ching wondered. Impossible to tell, of course, without knowing the range.

"What's the range on it?" he inquired.

"Two miles, First Agent," the voice of the tracker said.

"Impossible!" exclaimed Schneeweiss. "At that range, the thing couldn't be more than ten yards in diameter at this magnification. Check your figures!"

There was a period of silence, during which the course of the intruder changed. It no longer appeared to be growing larger; it had apparently swung into orbit about the asteroid, perhaps one mile out. The red ovoid swung over their heads, down behind their backs, under their feet, up in front of them again, overhead, behind, below. . . . An unnaturally fast orbit, Ching thought, one that can't be accounted for by the neutral laws of astrophysics.

"Range—.97 miles," the voice of the tracking officer said. "We've double-checked. It's in orbit around the asteroid, and a damned fast orbit too. It must be powered. It's got to be a ship."

"It *can't* be a ship!" Schneeweiss insisted. "It's far too small."

"Give us maximum screen magnification," Robert Ching ordered.

For a vertiginous moment, the "space" in which they floated seemed to swirl, go vague. Then the viewscreen image coalesced again. The far-off stars were still points of light, the empty black of space was still black emptiness. Nothing seemed to have changed, except. . . .

Except that the thing orbiting the asteroid was now revealed as a metallic red ovoid, perhaps twelve yards in diameter, with a ring of lenses circling its middle and a short coil of blue metal at its rear end.

"Do you realize what that is?" Schneeweiss shouted as the metallic egg swung beneath their feet again, in front, overhead. . . . "It's the same kind of craft we saw on the film, but much smaller. It . . . it must've followed our probe back!"

"From Cygnus!" Felipe exclaimed.

"From the stars!"

"We're getting something on the radio!" the voice of the tracking officer said. "On the hydrogen wave-length band."

"The logical universal wave-length for interstellar contact!" Schneeweiss exclaimed.

"Pipe it in here," Ching ordered.

Crackles, hisses, and then a strange, irregular pulsing, a series of beeps and pauses, could be heard as the red ovoid continued to circle them. Ching had the uncanny feeling, caused, he realized, by the illusion that this room at the core of the asteroid was actually in empty space, that the thing was watching them as they watched it, that it could somehow hear them as they listened to its radio pulsing.

"Beep-beep-beep. Pause. Beep. Pause. Beep-beep-beep-beep. Pause. Beep. Pause. Beep-beep-beep-beep-beep-beep." Then a much longer pause. And then the pattern repeated. "Beep-beep-beep. Pause. Beep. Pause. Beep-beep-beep-beep. Pause. Beep. Pause. Beep-beep-beep-beep-beep-beep." Another longer pause, and the pattern began repeating again.

"What is it?" Ching said. "It sounds somehow familiar. . . ."

"Three . . . one . . . four . . . one—six. . . ." Schneeweiss muttered distractedly to himself. "Three, one, four, one, six! Of course!" he shouted. "It's pi! Pi to four decimal places, repeated over and over again. The ratio of the circumference of a circle to its diameter! It's telling us it understands our mathematics! It's telling us it knows our number system has a decimal base."

"It's telling us it exists and is the product of intelligence," Robert Ching said. "It's telling us it knows we're sentient beings too."

Suddenly, the red ovoid broke orbit, began to accelerate rapidly, outward toward the orbit of Pluto. The disc rapidly shrank as the alien probe receded. Ching did not have to ask to know that it was receding in the direction of the 61 Cygnus system. Then, abruptly, while still showing a discernable disc, the red alien seemed to shimmer for a moment, then vanished.

They were alone, alone with the images of the thousands of stars that filled the blackness in which they floated.

But alone no longer, Robert Ching thought as he stared at the thousands of points of light, red, blue, white, yellow, that were the stars. It was as if each point of light were an eye looking at him—and he knew that the illusion was not far from the truth. For now those points of light were dead shining things no longer. They were the abodes of thousands of civilizations as far as he could see, and further, civilization upon civilization, forever, without end.

The universe had at last revealed its true face to Man, a face with a million eyes, a countenance vast and infinite, a face of limitless wonder, infinite variety. . . .

Robert Ching gazed upon the face of the universe.

And the face he saw, the face that stared back, the glorious, infinite face, was the Face of Chaos.

8

Boris Johnson, dressed in anonymous Maintenance coveralls, stood in the square of greenery immediately across the
small static street from the entrance to the Mercurian Ministry of Guardianship building. The Ministry itself was the
tallest structure on Mercury, except for the environment
dome itself, and its white plasteel facade soared nearly to
the heavily polarized permaglaze of the dome above it, outside of which the thin but caustic Mercurian atmosphere
raged—instant death lurking outside the dome, making it a
cage far more perfect than anything the Hegemony alone
could construct. With this area of the planet now on the
dayside, where it would remain for the next sixty days as
Mercury completed its leisurely revolution about its own
axis, not much shorter in duration than its orbit around the
sun, the blazing solar furnace, so nearby, could dimly be
seen even through the all-but-opaqued permaglaze, remind-
ing all within the dome how frail and isolated they were,
how totally confined and artificial their bubble of safety was.

The square in which Johnson stood was itself an attempt
by the Hegemony to counter that feeling of impending destruction, of artificiality; a caged feeling that verged on claus-
trophobia. Only sixty yards by seventy, the square was an
expanse of real grass, rimmed by two score genuine oak trees,

both brought from Earth, planted and maintained at tremendous expense. It was no esthetic frill, but a psychological necessity on Mercury, this bucolic illusion in the permaglaze cage.

The park was jammed with Wards. It seemed to Johnson that every Ward not otherwise occupied in the dome was huddled there amidst the greenery, trying for the moment to forget that they were trapped in this cage on the most hostile planetary surface in the Solar System, with the exception of the gas giants.

And all to the good, Johnson thought as he felt the bulge of his lasegun in one coverall pocket, the smaller shape of the vial of nerve gas concentrate in another. There were perhaps three hundred Wards milling aimlessly about the park. Nearly a hundred and fifty of them were League agents, committed to risking their lives against terrible odds in the diversionary frontal attack on the Ministry building, designed to force the Hegemonic Council to seal off the Council Chamber and thus render themselves vulnerable to the real attack from within the Ministry itself.

Half an hour ago, there had been still more League agents among the Wards in the square, a good fifty more—men who were going willingly to certain death.

The wide plastomarble steps leading up to the Ministry had a constant trickle of Wards coming and going up and down them, for the Ministry was the busiest building on Mercury, with hundreds of Wards coming and going on one errand or another all day: obtaining travel passes, work permits, domicile authorizations—negotiating the maze of red tape which festooned the life of every Ward of the Hegemony from birth till death.

So it had been easy for those fifty agents to enter the building over a period of half an hour, one by one, among dozens of ordinary Wards. Now another agent entered the Ministry, Guilder, one of the six agents Johnson had picked to lead against the pumproom after the diversionary attacks began.

While the agents in the square attacked the Ministry from

without, the fifty agents in the building would sacrifice their lives to the lethal Beams by attacking the corridors surrounding the Council Chamber itself—a diversion within a diversion.

Boris Johnson didn't like sending fifty men to certain death, and had in fact kept this part of the plan secret from all but those who absolutely had to know, but with the stakes this high, there was just no room for squeamishness. The attack on the exterior of the building would be so obviously futile that the Council and the Guards would be sure to see it for the diversion that it was, and be on the lookout for a second, earnest, attack. They would take the sacrificial attack by the fifty men on the Council Chamber area as the true assassination attempt, and concentrate their attention on it.

They would not be likely to realize that this too was a diversion from the real assassination attempt until it was much too late. . . .

Fifty men would pay with their lives to destroy the Hegemonic Council, but Boris Johnson, while he felt regret, felt no guilt. Like everyone else involved with the mission, they were volunteers who knew exactly what they were doing.

Besides, Johnson had no illusions about his own chances of seeing another day. It would be possible to get into the pumproom, assassinate the Council, but after that . . . escape would be not much less than impossible.

But it would be well worth it. In one stroke, the entire leadership of the Hegemony would be destroyed. There would be chaos; in the confusion it might just be possible to escape. But everyone on this mission had to consider himself a dead man until the Council was dead. There was a certain freedom to be gained by considering yourself already dead. Every man had to die someday, and by thinking of today as that day, one was free to think of giving one's death meaning, of making it count. . . . Thoughts of survival could only be afforded after the mission was completed.

Now Johnson saw yet another League agent climb the Ministry steps and enter the building.

He checked his watch. The timing was critical and had to be precise. In twenty-seven minutes, the attack on the Ministry would begin. Two minutes later, the fifty agents scattered now throughout the Ministry to avoid notice would have to converge, by timing alone, on the ring of corridors surrounding the Council Chamber and launch the second diversion. At that moment, the attention of the Guards would be split between the frontal assault and the attack on the Council Chamber.

At that moment, Johnson and his six men would have to converge on the pumproom, innocuously, from different directions, without even hinting at an Unpermitted Act.

While inside the pumproom, Jeremy Daid would have to get the Guards to open the door no more than a few seconds after the agents converged outside—no more than five seconds after the convergence itself caused the Beams in the corridor to pop.

The need for utter precision, a precision that each man would have to achieve independently, was terrifying if you thought too hard about it. One piece of bad timing and the whole thing would be blown—the Guards would pop every Beam in the building manually if the Guardian didn't do it first.

Johnson checked his watch again. Twenty-five minutes to zero. He had estimated that it would take him nineteen minutes, proceeding with the necessary casualness, to get from the square to the pumproom door. Which meant that he should begin exactly six minutes from now. . . .

Johnson felt the tension rise within him as the seconds ticked slowly by. The plan demanded absolute perfection, and there were so many men involved, so many factors. It required an order more absolute than that of the Hegemony itself. . . .

Three minutes to go.

Johnson brushed his hands against the front of his coveralls, smoothing the cloth against his body, pushing the reassuring bulge of the lasegun against his hip.

One minute.

Johnson glanced up at the permaglaze dome high above him, saw the sun barely leaking through the nearly opaque plastic and knew that it was highly unlikely that he would ever see it again.

Now!

Boris Johnson sauntered slowly out of the square, crossed the street and began climbing the broad flight of steps that led up to the entrance to the Ministry of Guardianship. As he climbed, he took care not to move faster than the dozen or so Wards climbing the steps with him.

He reached the wide entrance portal at the top of the steps where two Guards stood to either side of the entranceway, sullenly studying the Wards as they entered the building. Johnson held his breath as he stepped past the Guards—a papers check at this point would throw the whole timing off. . . .

But the Guards looked through him as if he did not exist, and for once he was glad of their arrogant indifference.

Now he was in the big main lobby. There were two banks of elevators close by the entrance, both marked "Authorized Personnel Only." Eyes glared down at him from above the elevators banks, Beams sat there menacingly. Eyes and Beams ran along all four walls of the lobby at ten foot intervals. He had to check his watch to see if his timing was right, but it had to be a casual gesture.

He reached up, scratched his nose, passing his watch quickly before his eyes as he did so. Sixteen minutes to zero. So far, so good.

He walked slowly towards the big escalator at the rear of the lobby. Should use up two minutes now, he thought. He walked past Guards hurrying towards the elevators, ordinary Wards coming from the escalator, nodded to two Maintenance men as they passed him, and then he was at the escalator.

He hesitated at the base of the escalator, wondering if he could chance another look at his watch. Glancing upward at the Eye and Beam in the ceiling above the escalator, he decided against it.

Figuring that it was about fourteen minutes to zero, he boarded the escalator. Four flights to the pumproom floor. He had estimated about two minutes a flight.

The trip up the escalator seemed agonizingly slow, slower, so it seemed, that he had figured it to be. On each of the three intermediary landings, he had to resist a strong impulse to check his watch—but the Eyes and Beams overlooking every landing restrained him.

Finally, Johnson reached the fourth landing, stepped off the escalator. I've simply *got* to check the timing now, he thought. He glanced about the corridor in front of him with the air of a harried Ward late for an appointment with some malevolent minor Ministry official, and quickly checked his watch. An Eye on the wall observed him, passed the datum on to the Guardian. But apparently, the computer found the move innocuous, Johnson thought, noting with relief that he was still alive.

Five minutes to zero. Which gave him a little more than five minutes to get to the area of the pumproom door—and getting there too early would be as bad as getting there too late.

He started down the long corridor, past door after numbered door, Beam after Beam, Eye after Eye, tracing the path he had to follow in his mind: down to the end of this corridor, right turn, follow that corridor to the end, make a left, and then another fifty yards to the pumproom door.

Johnson walked slowly, feeling the Eyes of the Mercury Guardian on his neck, imagining that they could see the lasegun and the vial of nerve gas concentrate through his clothing, imagining that every Beam he passed was about to pop, imagining that he was walking too slowly, that it was suspicious, but knowing that being forced to wait around by the pumproom door for long minutes would certainly be fatal. . . .

A Guard passing him going in the opposite direction looked straight through him, two Maintenance men passed by, nodded, and then he passed a large cross-corridor which intersected his at right angles.

He saw Guilder, one of the agents of his six-man squad, coming down the cross-corridor, and another agent, Jonas, about ten yards behind him. He studiously ignored them, walked past the intersection without changing stride, knowing without looking that Guilder and Jonas were turning into the corridor behind him, following him towards the pumproom at long intervals.

Now he reached the end of the corridor, a T-intersection, turned right into a more crowded corridor, dozens of Wards, several Guards moving along it in both directions. Good! He and Guilder and Jonas would not form a pattern moving in the same direction through such a crowd . . . and yes, there was Wright, about twelve yards in front of him, moving past those two Guards. The individual paths were beginning to converge as planned.

Johnson continued along the corridor, increasing his pace slightly, so that he was beginning to gain ground on Wright, and by the time he had reached the next T-intersection, Wright was only about eight yards ahead of him. He paused for a moment as Wright turned left, risked a quick glance at his watch—three minutes to zero.

Johnson turned left, continued to close with Wright, who was now slowing his pace somewhat. As he made the turn, he was able to see that Guilder and Jonas were only about six yards apart now, and that Guilder, the foremost, was making the turn less than eight yards behind him. It was coming off! They were all converging perfectly!

He looked down the long corridor, saw Eyes and Beams along both walls at regular ten-foot intervals, door after white-painted door. About thirty yards down, he could see one dark door, naked dull-gray lead plating, with a red sign above it that he knew read "Authorized Personnel Only" and an Eye and Beam directly below the sign—the pumproom.

Beyond the pumproom, at the far end of the corridor, he saw two men coming toward him on the opposite side, the side on which the pumproom door was located—Poulson and Smith, with perhaps ten yards between them and the gap slowly closing. And now Ludowiki turned the corner, not five yards behind Smith! Perfect! Perfect!

Johnson increased his pace as Wright slowed down, timed it so that he and Wright and Poulson and Smith and Ludowiki would all come together outside the pumproom door at the same time, less than two minutes from now, with Guilder and Jonas catching up to him at the same moment. . . .

Now, Johnson thought, just about *now*, the men in the square should be charging across the street and up the ministry steps. He could see it in his mind's eye. . . .

The agents in the park suddenly charging as one man through the crowd of Wards, bowling some over, perhaps, panicking the rest. . . . The hundred and fifty League agents reaching the base of the steps, laseguns drawn, firing at random, perhaps getting halfway up the steps unopposed before Guards erupted from the main Ministry entrance. . . .

And the furious gunbattle that must now be raging between the League agents and the Guards, bodies blackening, rolling down the steps, Wards screaming, running for cover, the air filling with the sickening, sweet smell of charred flesh. . . .

And above him, the Council Chamber being sealed off, while in the pumproom, now only a dozen yards in front of him, the pumps whirring into life, feeding life-giving air into the Council Chamber as they would feed death in another few minutes. . . .

Any moment now, Johnson thought, as he came within ten yards of the pumproom door, as Wright slowed to a near-halt but five yards in front of him, as he saw Smith and Poulson and Ludowiki near the pumproom door, as he heard Guilder's and Jonas' footsteps close behind him, the second diversion should begin. . . .

He visualized the fifty League agents suddenly bursting into the corridors surrounding the Council Chamber above him. He could all but see the scores of Beams popping, the ring of corridors becoming deathtraps of radiation, his men falling, willingly giving their lives in the cause of Democracy as. . . .

He and the six agents converged just outside the pump-room door. He imagined the image being picked up by the Eye above the lead door, being relayed to the Guardian deep in the nether bowels of the Ministry. . . .

Johnson whipped out his lasegun, saw his six men doing the same.

Then he heard a quick series of tiny explosions and dull clicks as plugs were blown from Beams all along the corridor, fell to the floor. He saw the plug of the Beam above the pumproom door burst outward ahead of a puff of white smoke, and he knew that invisible, deadly radiation was flooding the corridor, and then. . . .

Vladimir Khustov looked contentedly around the Council Chamber—at the white-paneled walls concealing a foot of lead, at the small grills along the baseboards through which air could be pumped, at the tv monitor before him on the walnut table, at the portable control-console-communicator beside it, at the silvery tanks with their regulator in the far corner of the room. Khustov smiled contemptuously as he scanned the nervous faces of his fellow Councilors, at the bland, robotlike mask that was the face of Constantine Gorov, at that cretin Torrence, pouring himself still another bourbon from the carafe on the silver tray in the center of the Council table.

Khustov laughed, poured himself a small vodka, sipped at it, savoring the sting of it on his lips.

"I fail to see the humor of this situation, Vladimir," Torrence whined, downing half his drink at one gulp. "We've spotted scores of known League agents outside the Ministry and we can assume that they're armed. And more of them inside the building itself. The whole place is crawling with League agents, and plan or no plan, I don't like it."

Coward! Khustov thought contemptuously. Torrence is worse than a coward, he's an anachronism, a creature better suited to the ghastly millennium before the Hegemony, when we were divided up into hundreds of nations, each one at the others' throat—that's when he belongs. A fool can see that Jack only serves Order because in this age it's his only path to power. He doesn't understand Order at all. If he did, he'd understand the futility of opposing it; he doesn't understand how futile the League's attempt is because he can't really believe that all is under absolute control. He probably doesn't even believe that complete Order is possible—or he wouldn't waste his time and effort in endless political maneuvering. If he really understood the Hegemony, he'd realize that the whole structure, the Guards, the Guardians, *everything*, is aligned *against* him and *for* me.

By serving Order, by insuring peace and prosperity, Vladimir Khustov knew that he also served himself—for the entire Hegemony, every planet and rock that men would ever see, every last Ward, was a pattern of absolute, unchanging Order, and he, Khustov, was at its center. He served the Order well, and the Order reciprocated. It was the best of all possible worlds, and no Torrence could upset it. . . .

"The plan," Khustov said evenly, "is totally foolproof. The Guards are waiting for those League agents in the square and I guarantee not one of them will gain the Ministry entrance—and if they did, what good would it do them? How could they possibly expect to fight their way through a whole building filled with Eyes and Beams and Guards?"

"That's the whole point," Torrence said, downing the rest of his bourbon and pouring himself another in one continuous motion. "Not even Johnson's stupid enough to believe that *those* men could actually accomplish anything. So they've got to be a diversion, a decoy. It's the other League agents, the ones in the building, that worry me. Who knows what they're up to? You're playing it too cagy, Vladimir. We know that there are at least forty League agents in the building, and some of them are pretty high up in the League hierarchy. Why don't we just play it safe and pop every damned Beam in the whole building and get 'em for sure right now?"

"I'm surprised," Khustov said, "that you, Jack, with your . . . uh . . . propensity for finessing, can't see through Johnson's finesse. The men outside the building are obviously there to make us believe that the men *in* the Ministry, when they attack, are the real thing. But just as obviously, if you think about it, Johnson must know that the men in the building can't accomplish anything either. What can they do, try to storm this Council Chamber? The moment that happens, the Chamber is sealed off and the corridors surrounding us are flooded with radiation. We could be safe without a single Guard in the entire building, and Johnson has to know it. So it's a double-finesse—*both* groups are decoys."

"But what's the point?" Torrence said. "Who cares whether they're decoys or not? Let's just kill 'em!"

"The point," Khustov said, "is that we're after bigger game. I want Johnson himself, and I want him alive. There is much to be learned from studying him under . . . the, ah, *proper investigatory procedures*. I want to destroy the Democratic League, but I want to go further. I want to learn why men persist in such insanity so that measures can be taken to insure that no such organization will ever form again. We're very close to total control. We already control environment. The next logical step is to control heredity. I hope that we may learn enough from studying the correlations between Johnson's mind and his genetic makeup to be able to breed such rebelliousness out of the race. Then Order will *really* be total."

"Here you are babbling about Order and control," Torrence sneered, "and what are you doing? You're risking our lives as bait. And you're betting them on being able to read Johnson's mind! How can you be so sure? What about what Gorov would call 'random factors?' "

"He has a point," Gorov said. "Your plan is internally sound—yet it *does* depend on knowing exactly what Boris Johnson plans to do. Perhaps. . . ."

Khustov laughed arrogantly. Fools! he thought. Even Gorov, who at least should know better.

"I'll prove it to you all, if it'll make you feel any better," he said. "Gather around this monitor, and I'll show you exactly what the League is up to. Even *you* ought to believe your own eyes, Jack."

Muttering, and with Torrence grimacing and taking his drink with him, the Councilors arose, and gathered in front of the monitor, flanking Khustov.

"I've had this hooked into the Guardian circuit so we can see anything any Eye in this building sees," Khustov said. He flipped a switch on the control console, pressed one of several score buttons on the face of the device. The television screen showed a view of the park opposite from the Ministry as seen by an Eye high up on the facade above the entrance.

"Here we have Johnson's outside men," Khustov said, "Safely hidden in a crowd of Wards—or so they think. But of course, they've underestimated the data banks of the Guardian. Enough of them are on the records here to show up as Hegemonic Enemies in a thorough facial check-out. They will no doubt make the first move, and then. . . ."

Khustov pressed another button, and now the screen showed a crowded corridor somewhere within the Ministry. "The agents *here* . . ." he said, and changed the view again to show another, similar corridor. "And here. . . ." Yet another corridor. "And here . . . and so forth, will begin the second diversion, an all-out attempt to storm the Council Chamber. And probably at that very moment, Mr. Boris Johnson. . . ."

Khustov changed the view again, and now the screen showed the pumproom door, and perhaps ten feet of corridor on either side of it. A collective gasp went up from the Councilors gathered around the monitor, for Boris Johnson himself had just appeared in the field of vision of the Eye that the screen was now connected to.

"The Beam! The Beam! Blow the Beam!" Torrence shouted. "We've got him! What're you waiting for?"

"I told you," Khustov said. "I want him alive. . . . Look at that—more League agents converging on the pumproom. Now even you can see that he's doing exactly what I said he would, Jack. Two diversionary attacks, and then Johnson and those few men break into the pumproom. The attacks cause us to seal the Council Chamber, and then Johnson drops some gas into the air line. One must admire Johnson's courage, I suppose—were it not based on such utter stupidity. No doubt he is counting on his agent Daid in the pumproom to get the door open for him before the radiation in the corridor can kill him and his men, after the Beam pop."

"And of course you've removed Daid?" Cordona said.

"Quite the contrary," replied Khustov. "Daid will be permitted to get the door open so that Johnson can walk right into our little mousetrap."

Khustov switched over to the outside Eye again. "Now all we do is wait," he said. He and the Councilors idly surveyed the scene in the square for a few moments.

Suddenly, a wave of men charged out of the crowd of Wards, across the street toward the Ministry steps.

Khustov laughed. "The trap is about to be sprung," he said, throwing a switch on his control console. "I've just sealed off the Council Chamber. We're on internal air supply now, just as Johnson wanted. However. . . ."

He threw another switch. "And now," he said, "I've sealed off the air lines from the pumproom. We're as self-contained in this Chamber now as if we were in a spaceship."

Khustov walked quickly over to the tanks in the corner of the room, fiddled with the regulator.

"There," he said smugly. "We've got enough air in these tanks for two hours. Now let Mr. Boris Johnson do his worst. He's quite finished."

As the plugs of the Beams in the corridor popped, as he stood with his six men by the pumproom door, lasegun drawn, Boris Johnson tried to think only of what should now be going on inside. Seconds ago, Daid should've yelled to one of the Guards that he heard someone trying to break into the pumproom. The Guard would've grumbled no doubt, but he surely would feel constrained to check. Any moment now, the door should swing open. Any second . . . and if the door *didn't* open in another second or so—

The lead door opened a crack, began to slowly swing inward. As soon as it was open wide enough, Johnson jammed his foot inside.

He heard a curse from the other side of the door, then felt the pressure of someone trying to close the door on his foot; then he and four of the agents crashed against the door with the full weight of their bodies.

The door flew open, revealing a dazed Guard sprawled on his behind in the doorway, lasegun still in hand.

Before the Guard could move, Johnson and four or five of the others caught him with lasebeams. His body was burnt to a heap of loose black ashes in a fraction of a second, and as the heap of ashes began to disintegrate, the agents rushed into the pumproom, and Wright, the last one inside, slammed the lead door shut behind them.

Safe! Johnson thought. Home free! We're inside and we're alive!

He took a quick, deep breath and surveyed the situation. The pumproom was small; maybe twelve by twenty feet. There was a battery of pumps along the far wall opposite the door with five stunned men in Maintenance coveralls standing by them. The short, wiry man looking on knowingly must be Daid.

Between the door and the pumps was an untidy collection of crates, metal boxes, spare parts and assorted junk. Between the pumps and the piles of equipment five Guards stood watching the technicians. As the door was slammed, they had whirled, drawn their laseguns, and for an idiotic, timeless moment, Guards and League agents stood facing each other.

Johnson hit the floor in a diving roll, firing as he fell. A Guard screamed, blackened, went down as Johnson met the floor and rolled behind a large metal box. He heard a scream behind him, looked back and saw that Guilder had been hit—his whole arm and half his right shoulder burned away.

The other League agents had hit the deck, rolled behind the sparse cover, and were firing away at the exposed Guards. Another Guard screamed, burned and fell as two lasebeams converged on his chest.

The three remaining Guards dove for the floor, tried to protect themselves by keeping the League agents pinned down behind the crates and machinery.

Johnson saw lasebeams hit the front of the metal box behind which he crouched, felt it heat up as two of the Guards concentrated their fire on it.

Then he heard another scream. Ludowiki had run from cover at the three Guards; he had been hit in the left shoulder. He crumpled and fell, but as he fell, he caught one of the Guards flush in the face with a searing red lasebeam. The Guard's head vanished in a cloud of black, oily smoke. Jonas jumped from cover as the two remaining Guards momentarily turned their attention to Ludowiki.

Jonas and one of the two remaining Guards caught each other with almost identical shots—in the neck. Neither had time to scream as their charred heads fell from blasted necks.

Johnson rolled from cover and caught the last prone Guard between the shoulder blades with a lasebeam. The Guard gave one short, shrill scream and then the pumproom was quiet.

Johnson stood up, ran to the pumps. Smith, Wright and Poulson, the three surviving agents, followed him.

The five technicians stared at the armed men in a disbelieving daze. Jeremy Daid rushed forward. "Good work!" he shouted. "We've done it! We've done it!"

Johnson ignored Daid for the moment, turned to the cowering Maintenance men. "Behave yourselves, and no one gets hurt," he barked. "One of you makes a move, we kill you all."

He turned to Daid. "The air lines!" he said.

Daid nodded wordlessly, led him to the bank of pumps.

Thin lead pipes led from the top of the center pump up to the ceiling and through it. "This one feeds air to the Council Chamber," Daid said, pointing to the center pump.

Johnson took the vial of nerve gas concentrate from his pocket. "How do I. . . ?"

Daid pointed to a fine-meshed wire grill on the face of the pump. "This is the intake duct," he said. "Dump it in here, and I'll close it off with this plastiseal. The pump'll suck pure nerve gas into the air lines."

Johnson uncorked the vial, spilled the liquid inside into the duct. Immediately, it began to vaporize, and the vapor was sucked into the pump. Daid slapped the sheet of plastiseal over the opening. The suction of the pump pulled the plastic sheet against the duct mouth, sealing it shut.

"We've done it!" Johnson shouted. "The gas should be hitting them right now!"

He grinned at his men. "We've killed the entire Hegemonic Council! That stuff works instantly. They should be all dead by now!"

"At last," Wright began, "We've—"

"Look!" Smith shouted, pointing to the door. The heavy lead door was beginning to glow red-hot.

"The Guards!" Poulson shouted. "They're burning through the door.

Johnson felt a sickening, sinking sensation in his stomach. He had anticipated this moment from the beginning, but now it was really upon him. Now he was facing certain death only moments after total victory, trapped in a room from which there was no escape, the Guards burning down the door with laseguns, the corridor beyond filled with deadly radiation. . . . He found that he really wanted very much to live, now that there was so much more to live for.

Johnson stared woodenly at the door. The whole door was now glowing cherry red, and he could feel the heat clear across the room. But there was something in the back of his mind, something that. . . .

"Of course!" he suddenly shouted. "If they're burning through the door, it means they must've sealed the Beams outside! If we can get past those Guards, maybe we can escape after all!"

He watched the door. The metal around the hinges was beginning to sag, to run like warm putty. . . .

"Let's get some cover!" he ordered. "Hit 'em as they come in."

He motioned the five terrified technicians behind a pile of crates with his lasegun. The Maintenance men went prone behind the crates, too scared to move. Johnson himself crouched down behind some kind of spare ductwork lying in front of the bank of pumps. Daid scooped up one of the laseguns of the slain Guards, then joined the others.

Johnson and his men trained their laseguns on the door. The metal around the hinges was really flowing now, and the whole door was sagging inward.

"They'll be sitting ducks as they come in," Johnson said. "Open up as soon as the door falls and stand your ground. We've got cover here, and we can keep 'em out of this pumproom for quite a while. If we can cut down all the Guards in the corridor as they come in, we've got a small chance. They'll have to reset the Beams in the corridor at the very least. Maybe the Beams in the rest of the building have been blown too. If they have, we may be able to fight our way to the street. . . ."

Johnson could not quite make himself believe what he was saying. Escape from the Ministry was almost certainly impossible. But at least they could go down fighting. They could take dozens, maybe scores of Guards with them. This would be a day that the Hegemony would remember and shudder at for as long as the tyranny endured, and perhaps it would ignite the Wards to—

The door bulged crazily inward. There was a sigh of metal, and the hinges gave way in a shower of molten lead, and the pumproom door crashed to the floor, spattering lead droplets into the air from its semiliquid far side.

Instinctively, Johnson and his men were firing blindly and furiously as the door fell. But their lasebeams seared empty air—no targets, no Guards appeared in the doorway.

Then the air beyond the doorway was no longer empty. A heavy red mist billowed through the doorway, surged toward them, a great cloud of the stuff being pumped in under heavy pressure.

It advanced toward them in a solid front. Johnson leapt up, with the others following him, backed up against the bank of pumps at the rear of the room, as the breathable air was inexorably forced back, back, constricted into an ever more limited area by the heavy red gas.

Johnson felt protuberances on the pump dig into his back, as he flattened himself against it, as the entire room filled with the gas.

Then he was enveloped, blinded by the heavy red mist. Futiley, instinctively, he held his breath until his lungs began to ache. He fought against the ever-growing pain in his chest, fought not to breath, fought and fought and fought until he could fight the reflexes of his own body no longer.

With a great shuddering sigh, he released the carbon dioxide in his lungs, exhaled deeply. . . .

And the red gas immediately forced itself into his lungs, a heavy, choking syrupy stuff that seemed to flow like molasses down his throat, through his nostrils, into his lungs, his stomach, his very bloodstream. . . .

He felt himself inundated in a vast velvet sea of treacle. . . . His vision began to go dim, his knees turned to jelly. Then the blackness enclosed him. He felt himself falling, falling, falling, a fall with no bottom that seemed to last forever. . . . He felt his consciousness fading as his body fell, whirling away into a cold black pit. . . .

He fought against it for a few wan moments, and then the last of his will evaporated, and he was a tiny mote, fading, fading, drifting away into blackness, void. . . .

Nothingness.

"The servant of Order strives to force his enemy to accept the unacceptable. To serve Chaos, confront your enemy with the unacceptable— and he will eagerly choose any lesser evil you desire to make unavoidable."

Gregor Markowitz,
Chaos and Culture

9

A swirl of blackness eddying the dark void. . . . A vortex of nothingness a shade less profound than the ocean of nonbeing in which he swam. . . .

Then the tactile sensation of firmness, of some substance beneath his buttocks and against his back. His body was seated in something. . . a chair. . . .

A moment of utter ecstasy seared through the clouded mind of Boris Johnson. I'm alive! he thought. Somehow, somewhere, I'm alive! Alive! Alive! *Alive!*

Then his vision began to clear, and a big white balloon floated in front of him, a balloon with long black hair . . . a balloon that smiled down at him. . . .

His vision went sharp, and his heart sank as his eyes focused on the face smiling down at him.

"So we meet at last," said Vladimir Khustov.

"You . . . you're alive!" Johnson stammered foolishly. He stared wildly around the room he found himself in. He saw the big walnut table before him, and the men seated around it . . . Gorov, Torrence, the whole Hegemonic Council staring at him, studying him as if he were some strange bug. . . . They're all alive! he thought. I've failed, failed miserably! But how . . . ? *How?*

Khustov laughed. "I see you're somewhat confused," he said. "You expected us to be dead, eh? And no doubt when the gas overcame you, you thought you were dying yourself. But as you can see, the gas was an innocuous anesthetic, as innocuous as your own foolish plot, and we are all of us alive. Is not the surprise, in the balance, a pleasant one?"

"But how . . . ? The nerve gas. . . ." Johnson mumbled forlornly. "You *can't* be alive. . . . You. . . ."

"Come, come, even *you* must believe your own senses," Khustov said. "We're all very much alive. Your own foolish pride in your supposed cleverness is what defeated you, Johnson. You actually thought that one of your agents in such a critical position as the pumproom would go unde-tected! A most peculiar psychology—a man who believes what he wants to believe. It was all a trap, Mr. Boris Johnson, and you walked right into it. Once we knew that Daid was a League agent, we knew that you could never resist trying to kill us all, once we made ourselves available. We let you think you had an edge, a secret weapon within the Ministry, but that very knowledge on your part was our weapon against you. We simply let you go through with your plan, and sealed off the Council Chamber, using an internal air supply instead of the pumproom lines, and then . . . but you know the rest."

Johnson was stunned beyond feeling even despair. The Hegemony had been ahead of him every step of the way! He had been such a fool, such a blind, utter fool!

"But why didn't you kill me, Khustov?" he said tiredly. "Surely you don't intend to let me go?"

Khustov seemed to be studying him earnestly. "Ah, but you're too *interesting* to merely kill," he said. "I don't un-derstand you, Johnson, and I want to. The Democratic League is through, utterly finished. Surely you realize that?"

Despite himself, despite his hate and loathing for Khus-tov and everything he stood for, Boris Johnson found himself nodding involuntarily in agreement. He *was* through, and the League *was* finished. But did it really matter? Had the League ever really had a chance? A handful of men against a government that ruled every square inch of the Solar System, every man, woman and child alive? He felt utterly futile, used up, even deluded. What made me do it in the first place? he wondered. How could I have believed it possible to destroy the Hegemony, with its Guardians and Guards, its bottomless resources, its total control. . . ?

"I see we at least agree on one thing," Khustov said. "The Democratic League is finished. It never was a serious threat, but I admit that you had a certain nuisance value. And there is no place for nuisances in the Hegemony of Sol. We must make certain that no such nuisance ever occurs again. That's why you're alive. I cannot understand why anyone would want to join a thing like the League in the first place, why anyone would want to disturb the Order of the Hegemony. And I want to understand this psychosis. We *must* understand it in order to breed it out of the race. Why, Johnson, why? I'm willing to listen. Tell me, just what in the world did you ever hope to gain?"

Johnson stared woodenly up at Khustov. What kind of question is that? he thought. It's self-evident—*isn't it?* Men will always fight for their freedom against tyranny, won't they? Even a tyrant like Khustov should be able to see that! Shouldn't he?

"The destruction of the Hegemony, of course!" Johnson snarled. "The end of this tyranny! Freedom for the human race!"

"The destruction of the Hegemony . . ." Khustov sighed, shaking his head. "But why? What would you replace it with?"

"With Democracy! With Freedom!"

Once again, Khustov shook his head incredulously. "But why?" he said. "What's wrong with the Hegemony? Are there wars that kill millions of people as in the Millennium of Religion and Nationality? No! The order of the Hegemony has brought true peace for the first time in human history! Are people starving? Do the Wards suffer plagues? No! Men have never been so prosperous and healthy. No one starves, no one is even poor. The word hardly has anything but an historical meaning anymore. Peace, plenty, prosperity—even contentment! You above all others should know that the Wards are content with the Hegemony. The League existed for ten years, and how many Wards were you able to recruit? A handful of fools and neurotics! And soon, even neurosis and stupidity will disappear. We'll breed them out of the race. We've brought about a utopia! Order is all but total, and soon it *will* be total. Then the Hegemony will rule absolute over every rock, every planet, that the human race will ever know. The entire Solar System will be a paradise, not for a year, or a century, or a millennium, but for as long as Man endures. Why should even a fool want to destroy this? We've given Man everything he needs! What else is there?"

Despite his feeling of being totally drained, despite the knowledge that the very worst had already happened, Boris Johnson was surprised to learn that he could still feel shock. *Khustov meant it!* He meant every word of it! He didn't think of himself as a tyrant—he was utterly sincere! It was the ultimate tyranny, the final triumph of total despotism—the despot himself was a prisoner of the system. He couldn't even see that. . . that. . . .

"Is that all there really is, Khustov?" he said. "You *really* believe that? What about Freedom?"

"Well what about it?" Khustov said blandly. "What is it but a word? Freedom from *what?* From disease, from poverty, from war? We've already achieved that. Or do you mean freedom *to?* To starve? To kill? To suffer? To wage war? To be unhappy? What is this freedom? What but a meaningless, obsolete word! What a fool you are, to throw your life away for a word!"

"It's not just a word!" Johnson insisted shrilly. "It's . . . it's. . . ."

"Well?" said Khustov. "What is it then? Do you know? Can you tell me? Can you even tell yourself?"

"It's . . . it's Democracy . . . when the people have the government they want. When the majority rules. . . ."

"But the people already have the government they want!"

Khustov exclaimed. "They want the Hegemony. The Wards are happy." He glanced at Jack Torrence, who was watching the proceedings with a sour grimace on his face. "Could it simply be," he said, "that *you* want to rule for your own pleasure, like . . . like certain others I could name? Isn't that it, Johnson? Isn't that really it? Aren't *you* the one who wants to be a tyrant? Aren't you the one who wants to thwart the desires of the Wards? Don't you want to force on them something they don't want?"

Johnson was silent. Khustov had to be wrong! Freedom was . . . *right*. The Hegemony was . . . *wrong*. Anyone could see that! *Couldn't they?* It just *was!* But . . . but . . .

But Vladimir Khustov had opened a yawning pit before him. He had never thought that his will to overthrow the Hegemony could have *personal* motivations before. He *knew* that Freedom and Democracy were right, and the absolute rule of the Hegemony wrong, he had always known, and he still felt it, deep in his guts.

But for the life of him, he could not verbalize his reasons, even to himself. Had his whole life been a lie? Was Khustov right? Had he thrown it away over nothing?

Why? Why? Why?

Arkady Duntov winced in the cruel glare, polarized the face-plate of his spacesuit even darker. It was hot in the suit— even this specially modified spacesuit couldn't keep a man alive on the Mercurian dayside for more than four hours.

But four hours would be more than long enough.

Duntov half-turned, looked behind him. Ten men stood in the harsh black shadow of the ship, dark clumsy figures in heavy spacesuits, the helmet visors all but opaqued. Lase-guns hanging in holsters from their belts, two of the men carrying large backpacks. He motioned to his men and they started forward to join him—radio silence must be maintained until the time for the ultimatum came. The whole mission had been gone over a thousand times, and by now even hand signals were hardly necessary.

Duntov checked the straps holding the powerful auxiliary transceiver to the back of his spacesuit, and then plodded heavily forward into a nightmare landscape.

Everywhere were great cliffs of jagged rock, huge solitary boulders eroded into twisted crazy shapes by the thin atmosphere of partially ionized gasses. The ground, if one could call it that, was littered with millions of rock splinters cracked from the cliffs and boulders by the alternating blistering heat of the Mercurian day and the bitter cold of the Mercurian night. Treacherous ponds of powdered rock alternated with pits of molten lead under the cruel glare of the nearby solar furnace, which, if looked directly upon, even through a heavily polarized visor, would burn out a man's retinas in a moment.

Duntov led his men through a narrow defile between two sheer cliffs, sidestepping a pool of lead that bubbled torpidly just beyond the mouth of the canyon. The suit temperature was rising, inching towards the unbearable.

The Mercurian surface, Duntov thought, the most inhospitable place in the Solar System that men could walk on. Only the surface of a gas giant could be more deadly. . . .

And, he thought, all the better for us.

He reached the far end of the canyon, and looked down and across a broad, saucerlike plain—perhaps what was left of some huge impact crater. In the center of the huge depression, amidst giant eroded boulders, pits of molten lead, millions of rock splinters, like a great pearl in a garbage heap, sat the hemispherical permaglaze environment dome that was the sole habitation of men on Mercury. The monstrous sun, upon which Duntov dared not gaze, turned the permaglaze dome into a shining bubble of bleak fire, a defiant, synthetic, human thing in a lifeless inferno.

And hence, terribly, utterly vulnerable. The dome had only two airlocks—the main one, at the far side of the dome and out of sight, servicing the small spaceport, and another that Duntov could make out directly ahead of him, an emergency exit that was a gesture of futility, for if the dome was holed, every human being on Mercury would face swift and certain death. No doubt, Duntov thought, the second airlock was there simply to allow access to the spaceport in case something happened to the primary lock.

The outer airlock entrances would be guarded, for such was the paranoiac thoroughness of the Hegemony that they would guard even these exits to oblivion, entrances through which there was no one to pass—but they would be guarded lightly.

Duntov made a hand signal to his men as they trudged out onto the plain and towards the dome. The party split up: seven men began circling the dome towards the spaceport airlock on the other side, while the other three followed Duntov around pools of lead and powdered-rock quagmires towards the auxiliary lock.

Duntov halted them at a jumble of boulders about twenty-five yards from the airlock. He crouched down behind a small boulder, motioned for his men to take cover.

He peered out over the top of the boulder at the airlock, a short hemicylindrical tunnel projecting out from the side of the dome like the entrance to an igloo. Two men in space-suits idled by the sealed airlock door at the blunt end of the hemicylinder. Only two! A piece of cake! Duntov thought as he unholstered his lasegun and trained it on the man to the left.

He gestured to his men. At this prearranged signal, one of them aimed his lasegun at the man Duntov was covering while the other two covered the right-hand Guard.

Duntov held his free left hand over his head and waited. This had to be timed right. He had to give the other party time to reach the main airlock before seizing this one, or the plan would be given away and the Guards at the main airlock, who probably would be more numerous, alerted.

Strictly speaking, it was not actually essential to control both locks—but if the Guards maintained control of either one, they might be able to send a large force against the other across the Mercurian surface before the Council capitulated. He would then be forced to go through with the killing of the entire population of the dome, a prospect he did not relish. . . .

So Arkady Duntov waited long minutes, reaiming his lasegun occasionally as his target shifted position, waited as the suit temperature continued to rise, as rivulets of sweat began to trickle down onto his face. . . .

Three . . . five . . . ten . . . fifteen minutes.

That should do it, Duntov thought. They're either in position now, or they'll never be. . . .

He jerked his chin against the pad inside his helmet, turning on his suit transceiver. "Mouse!" he said crisply, trying to make the break in radiosilence as brief as possible.

"Trap!" came the countersign, crackling with solar static. Duntov turned off the transceiver. *Now!* he thought.

He dropped his left hand. Four laseguns fired; blazing red beams of light, momentarily brighter than even the nearby glowering sun, lanced out simultaneously.

The two Guards were hit immediately, puffs of air wafting visibly out of the holes burnt into their suits. They fell, mortally wounded by the lasebeams, cooked within their suits by the terrible Mercurian heat as well.

Still maintaining radio silence, Duntov leapt up, led his men across the rubble strewn surface to the airlock. Duntov studied the great heavy door on the blunt end of the airlock. Burning through it would not be easy. Perhaps—the Brotherhood's information had not been that complete—there was a way to open the door from the outside. . . ?

Yes! That looks like it! he thought, spotting the single stud set in a small panel on the frame of the massive door.

Duntov pressed the stud and the door began to slide ponderously upward. He aimed his lasegun at the doorway, just in case, and as the door slid to a fully opened position—

A startled spacesuited Guard screwed his face into a mask of pain as the full glare of the sun blinded him through his unpolarized visor.

Duntov shot him in the midsection, then again, as he crumpled and fell, in the helmet. One of the men pressed a stud on an inside doorframe, and the door shut behind them.

We're inside! Duntov thought, as he waited for a minute while the airlock re-established its Earth-normal atmosphere. Then he cracked his helmet, swung the visor open and breathed deeply of the cooled air.

"Okay," he said, "set it up, Rogers."

The man carrying the backpack unstrapped it, withdrew a great wad of adhesoplastic explosive, and stuck it to the inner airlock door while the third man took a small detonator box from the pack, jammed its prongs into the explosive wad and then checked out a smaller box, a tiny radio transmitter. The explosive, Duntov knew, could be detonated from that small transmitter, or the one back on the ship, or the one the other party had, or both charges could be detonated by any one of the three.

"All set!" Rogers said.

Duntov unstrapped the powerful transceiver on his back, set it on the floor, tuned it to the Standard Internal Frequency of the Mercurian Ministry of Guardianship.

Then he spoke into his suit mike.

"Mousetrap One to Mousetrap Two! Mousetrap One to Mousetrap Two! Cheese One in position!"

A moment's silence, and then a static-distorted voice from the suit transceiver: "Mousetrap Two to Mousetrap One! Mousetrap Two to Mousetrap One! Cheese Two in position!"

The second explosive charge was in place in the main airlock. "Roger and clear," Duntov said. "Stand by."

"Okay," he muttered, turning on the auxiliary transceiver, "the Hegemony's got its rat, and now we've got ours!"

He unhooked the microphone from the transceiver, thumbed it on, and began to speak.

"I could of course have you killed," Vladimir Khustov said to the silent Boris Johnson. "Perhaps eventually I will. But if you cooperate, if you submit to depth psychoprobing willingly, perhaps you may be spared. Perhaps you can even be cured of your madness. If we can determine the exact nature of the psychosis that produces aberrant individuals such as yourself, it may be possible to correlate the disease with specific genetic traits, and by forbidding Wards carrying those genes to breed, eventually weed them out of the race. . . ."

Jack Torrence watched the whole sorry performance with a mixture of contemptuous amusement and disgust. It's a side of him I just never could understand, Torrence thought. Khustov the pedant—almost like Gorov, now. Khustov the fanatic. . . . Does Vladimir really believe all that swill? But he can't—after all, he's enough of a realist and a shrewd enough politician to've made himself Coordinator, and to keep himself in the catbird's seat—*so far*. A man like that's *got* to be a pragmatist, he can't actually believe all that garbage he's babbling. Sure, Vladimir has the best reason in the world to preserve the order of the Hegemony intact—he's at the top. I, on the other hand, Torrence conceded, would support any system that put me on top, no matter how many changes it brought about. Why not? The system exists to serve the ruler, not the other way around.

Vladimir must know that. . . .

Yet what ulterior motive can he have for this tiresome performance? What sane reason is there for keeping Johnson alive? Vladimir Khustov—fanatic. There ought to be some way of using that against him. . . .

"Haven't we listened to about enough of this, Vladimir?" Torrence finally said. "This farce is just a waste of time. Let's just dispose of Johnson and be done with it."

"I told you, we must study Johnson and his kind in order to—"

"Oh, come off it!" Torrence snapped. "First you're soft on the Brotherhood, now you don't want to kill Boris Johnson. Might I remind you that this man tried to kill both of us not so long ago?" He glanced around significantly at the other Councilors. "Might I also remind you that he just tried to kill us all? Are you getting squeamish, Vladimir? The Hegemony can ill-afford a squeamish Coordinator. . . ."

He studied the faces of the Councilors as he uttered the

last innuendo. Even Khustov's tame Councilors seemed to be wondering—and why not, since this man their boy now wanted to keep alive had just tried to murder them! Only Gorov seemed interested in Khustov's plans to "study" Johnson, and that idiot would study a maniac with a knife while he was being hacked to pieces.

Khustov, on the other hand, seemed really bugged. "I'm getting a little tired of you, Jack," he said. "Let me point out to the entire Council that my plan has worked perfectly every step of the way. Results are what count, and none of you can deny that results are what I've given you. Vice-Coordinator Torrence is very good at shooting off his mouth— I would be the last to deny that. But *results*. . . . That takes another kind of man entirely. I've been right so far, and I say we have very good reasons for—"

The communicator buzzer began to sound. Irritably, Khustov thumbed the audio on. "Well," he grunted, "what is it now. . . ?"

An unfamiliar voice filled the Council Chamber:

"This is an agent of the Brotherhood of Assassins. This is an agent of the Brotherhood of Assassins. Both airlocks of this environment dome are now under the control of the Brotherhood. We have placed powerful explosive charges in both airlocks. The charges are connected to dead man's switches. Any attempt to retake the airlocks will result in their instant detonation. You will be given seven minutes to verify the situation. At the end of that period, you will be given further orders. If those orders are not obeyed, or if any attempt is made to retake the locks, the charges will be detonated, the airlocks and adjacent portions of the dome blown apart and the interior of this dome exposed instantly to the conditions of the Mercurian surface. Everyone within the dome will be destroyed. You will now verify the situation and await further orders. Out."

The moment the communicator fell silent, everyone was shouting at once.

"What!"

"A bluff!"

"Send the Guards to the airlocks!"

"Seal the Council Chamber!" Torrence shouted, then realized that it would do no good. If the dome were holed, the entire environment control system would be destroyed by the terrible heat and hot caustic gasses. They might survive a bit longer in the sealed Chamber, but it would only be postponing the inevitable. . . . Of all the. . . !

Boris Johnson was laughing. "How does it feel?" Johnson crowed. "Caught in your own trap. The hunters become the hunted. The—"

"Enjoy yourself while you can!" Torrence said shrilly. "What makes you think the Brotherhood's on *your* side? They'll probably—"

"*Shut up!*" Vladimir Khustov roared, cutting through the tumult. Councilors, Torrence, even Johnson were cowed to silence. "We've got no time to yell and scream at each other," Khustov said. "We must act, and the first thing we must do is verify the situation. We could very well be faced with nothing more than a foolish bluff. . . ."

He turned to the communicator, spoke a few terse sentences in harsh, guttural Russian.

"You know that some of us don't speak Russian," Torrence whined, instantly suspicious. "What did you—?"

"I merely instructed the Commander of the Guards to attempt to establish contact with the men guarding the airlocks," Khustov said. "We should know in a moment if—"

A voice speaking breathless, excited Russian came through the communicator speaker, and Torrence had no need to understand the language to make out the meaning as Khustov's face creased in a heavy frown, as the Hegemonic Coordinator slammed a fist into a palm and cursed bilingually.

"It's no bluff," Khustov said in English. "The suit radios of all the airlock Guards are dead. The life systems telemetry channels are out too—the Guards can't be alive. No answers from the communicators inside the locks either. They've done it, all right!"

"But the *bombs* could be bluff . . ." Councilor Kuryakin

suggested wanly. "Maybe we should take the chance and storm the locks. . . ?"

"If they've captured the airlocks, there's no reason for them to be bluffing about the rest," Khustov said. "Time enough for desperation measures when we hear what their demands are. . . ."

The Councilors waited in stolid silence—like cattle in an abattoir, Torrence thought, his mind working feverishly. But all he could think of was how much he wanted to live. How insane the Brotherhood was. . . . What could they do? What way out was there? It couldn't all end this way. . . . It just *couldn't!*

Finally, the voice of the Brotherhood agent over the communicator broke the silence:

"You have now had ample time to verify the situation," the voice said. "You now know that you must follow our orders to the letter or die. You will be given exactly fifteen minutes to comply."

There was a dreadful, pregnant pause, and then the voice continued: "Your orders are as follows: Boris Johnson will be conducted to the emergency airlock and turned over to the Brotherhood of Assassins."

Another pause, during which the Councilors heaved great sighs of relief, and Johnson's face became a mask of utter confusion.

Jack Torrence all but laughed. Go figure the Brotherhood! he thought. They could kill us all—but all they want is Johnson! That's not so bad. A total victory becomes merely a partial one. That's not so bad at all. . . .

Then the voice spoke again: "Johnson will be accompanied by Councilor Constantine Gorov and Coordinator Vladimir Khustov. All three must be turned over to us at the emergency airlock, and they must arrive at the airlock alone. If there is the slightest hint of treachery, the main airlock will be instantly blown. If any attempt is made to follow us when we leave, the explosives will be detonated by remote control. You have fifteen minutes to comply, from my mark. If the three men are not in our hands by then, you are all dead men. *Mark! And out.*"

Khustov went pale. "I'll send every available Guard in the dome to the airlocks immediately!" he said. "We'll—"

"Just a minute!" Torrence snapped, his mind recovering from a moment of bewilderment. The Brotherhood taketh, he thought, and the Brotherhood giveth away! Blessed be the Brotherhood of Assassins!

"I don't think the lives of this Council and of everyone in the dome are yours to dispose of at will, Vladimir," Torrence said. "This is clearly a matter for the whole Council to decide. I demand a vote. I say we have to go along with the Brotherhood. What choice do we have? Either we all die, or we lose our prisoner and our good Councilor Gorov . . . and of course our treasured Coordinator. Two of us are taken prisoner, or we all die. The choice is obvious. Let's have a vote!"

Councilors nodded.

"We've got no choice!" Steiner said.

"He's right!"

"We can't resist."

"Wait! Wait!" Khustov screamed. "You can't do this to me! We can't knuckle under to threats! We've got to fight for—"

"I'm afraid the Vice-Coordinator is right," Gorov interrupted, in cold, even tones. "If we resist, we all die, you and I included, Vladimir. Even the two of us have nothing to lose by complying. Perhaps we won't be killed. It's literally impossible to predict the actions of the Brotherhood of Assassins. They never do the obvious."

Well, well, well! Torrence thought. Now there's an unexpected ally! Gorov's mad as a hatter. A human machine. . . . But that should clinch it. . . .

"Vote, gentlemen!" he said. "The ayes, please?"

"You can't do this!" Khustov screamed. "I'm the Coordinator! You can't do it!"

Torrence smiled. "And we're the Hegemonic Council,"

he said. "We elected you, and we can . . . er, decide your fate. Will all those in favor of complying with the ultimatum please say 'Aye'?"

"Aye!" "Aye!" "Aye!" "Aye!" "Aye!" "Aye!" "Aye!"

"Aye . . ." said Constantine Gorov.

"Aye!" Torrence said, with a broad grin. "The nays"?

"No!" Khustov howled. "No! No! No! No! No!"

"The ayes have it, nine to one," Torrence said. "I hereby declare the motion carried."

He bolted to his feet, half-leapt to the communicator. "Guards!" he ordered, as Khustov stared furiously at him in frustrated rage and fear. "Send a squad to the Council Chamber immediately. Their orders are to convey Boris Johnson, Councilor Gorov and . . . *former* Coordinator Khustov to the emergency airlock. . . ."

He turned to face the Council. "I think it would be wise to relieve Vladimir of his Coordinatorship temporarily, in order that the Guards not receive conflicting orders," he said. "Of course, if somehow Vladimir should be . . . ah, restored to us, he would reassume his position. But during the present emergency, I think it best that I assume the position of acting Hegemonic Coordinator. I trust there are no objections."

No Councilor spoke.

"Commander," Torrence said into the communicator, "you will inform all Guards that the powers of Coordinator Khustov have been suspended by the Hegemonic Council. You will inform them that Councilor Torrence is now acting Coordinator, and no one may countermand my orders— especially Councilor Khustov."

Torrence exulted as he waited for the Guards to arrive. Acting Coordinator! At last! And that "acting" will be easy enough to remove, with Vladimir out of the way. Hegemonic Coordinator Jack Torrence—ah, what a ring to it! There'll be changes made. . . . And if the Brotherhood ship should be intercepted—hmm, best idea would be to order it destroyed on sight. . . . There'll be changes made indeed!

"It is vain to search for solid ground on which to stand. The solid matter of the ground is, after all, but an illusion caused by a particular energy configuration—as is the foot which stands upon it. Matter is illusion, solidity is illusion, we are illusion. Only Chaos is real."

Gregor Markowitz,
The Theory of Social Entropy

10

Boris Johnson found himself walking mechanically down a corridor toward the airlock, flanked by Gorov and Khustov and all three of them surrounded by a phalanx of sullen Guards. As soon as they had left the Council Chamber, Khustov had ordered the Guards to return and arrest Torrence, but the Guards had not even bothered to refuse. They had simply ushered the three of them out of the Ministry and into a groundcar without a word, as if Khustov were no more than an ordinary Ward they had been ordered to dispose of.

Which, Johnson thought, he may very well now be. The Guards had no personal loyalties, only paranoia and absolute conditioned obedience to the will of whoever ran the Hegemonic Council. Khustov seemed to have realized this, for he had not said a word or tried to countermand Torrence's orders again during the entire trip across the dome to the airlock entrance.

Now, walking the last yards to the inner airlock door, surrounded by Guards, Khustov's shoulders dropped, his face was pale and lifeless; he seemed a broken man. In a sardonic way, Johnson found himself empathizing with the former Coordinator. Defeat snatched from the jaws of victory—they had both felt it in the past hour. And now they were both going to. . . .

To what? Johnson thought. The Brotherhood of Assassins makes no sense. They save Khustov, they save Torrence, and now they save me from the Hegemony . . . but they capture Gorov and Khustov too! Why Gorov? Why Khustov? Why me? Why *anything*?

Johnson found that he felt no fear. Having tasted victory, defeat and salvation in such rapid and dizzying succession, he could feel nothing at this point, nothing at all. His world, his life, was in ruins and now he was ready to face anything with a fearlessness born of total indifference. When you've got nothing, he thought, you've got nothing to lose.

Now they were about ten yards from the inner airlock door. The Guards halted, and the Captain brusquely shoved the prisoners forward. "We stay here," he grunted. "You go over to the intercom and tell 'em that you're here."

Johnson, Khustov and Gorov stood by the airlock door, not knowing which would be the least peculiar spokesman—Johnson, the prisoner of one side being handed over to the other; Khustov, the presumed enemy of the Brotherhood; or Gorov, who seemed to be in the same position as Khustov.

"Come on!" the Guard Captain shouted. "We've only got a few minutes left. One of you move!"

Johnson and Khustov glared at each other, as if each were daring the other to assume command of the situation. But it was Constantine Gorov who finally pressed the communicator stud and said: "This is Councilor Gorov. Johnson and Khustov are here with me."

"We are transferring the explosive from the inner airlock door to a wall so we can open it," a voice said through the intercom, a voice that, though distorted by the radio, seemed to Johnson strangely familiar. "The other bomb will remain in place and both can be detonated in a moment if there are any tricks. Any Guards that are with you must leave the corridor. If any Guards are visible when the airlock opens, we'll destroy the dome and everyone in it."

The Guards moved off with ill-concealed haste, disappeared around the corner of a cross corridor.

Then the inner airlock door slid up and open.

"Inside! Quickly!" a voice ordered from within.

Johnson, Gorov and Khustov entered the airlock, and the inner airlock door immediately slid shut behind them.

With his newfound indifference, Johnson noted the body of the slain Guard, the wad of plastic explosive stuck to a wall, the four spacesuited figures in the airlock. Then his capacity for shock was abruptly restored as he saw the face of the leader of the Brotherhood group through his spacesuit visor.

"Arkady!" Johnson croaked. "You! The Brotherhood. . . ."

It was the ultimate absurdity, the final demonstration of the futility of all he was, all he had been, all he had ever tried to do. Arkady Duntov a member of the Brotherhood! His most valued lieutenant, the man with all the plans! Arkady Duntov!

Things that had been mysteries suddenly became clear. How Duntov, who seemed so ordinary, had come up with so many complicated schemes. . . . How the Brotherhood had known of the League's plan to kill Khustov . . . and to kill Torrence . . . and to assassinate the Council. . . .

Old mysteries disappeared, revealing . . . only greater confusion! Why? Why? Why? What was the Brotherhood's game? What did all this mean. . . ?

"Why, Arkady, why?" he muttered.

Duntov, he saw, was looking straight at him, yet seemed to be staring through him. "No time for talk now, Boris," Duntov said. "Into those spacesuits." He pointed to the rack of empty suits along one wall of the airlock.

Johnson, Gorov and Khustov began to don the spacesuits. As Johnson pulled the helmet over his head and was about to close the visor, Duntov turned to him, met his gaze, and said, "I want you to know right now, Boris, in case . . . in case anything should go wrong, that though we've never really been on the same side, we've been fighting for the same things all along."

"How can you say that? After all the monkey wrenches the Brotherhood has thrown into our plans!"

"I wish I could tell you," Duntov said. "I wish I understood it more fully myself. But we'll be taking you to someone who can explain far better than I. Someone who . . . who I trust completely, who you can trust too. Robert Ching can make you understand. . . . Now let's get out of here!"

Duntov opened the outer airlock door, and Johnson winced at the cruel glare, even through his heavily polarized visor. The Brotherhood men formed a cordon around the prisoners and they set forth across the tortured Mercurian landscape.

Duntov led the party across the saucerlike plain on which the dome was built, skirting pools of molten lead, treacherous pits of powdered rock. As they neared the lip of the great depression, another Brotherhood party, seven men, joined them, and they all entered the mouth of a canyon which led into the jumbled, twisted hills that rimmed the plain.

They trudged on in silence, and Johnson barely noticed the fetid heat mounting inside his suit. It didn't seem to matter; nothing seemed to matter. He felt like the pawn of forces he could not see, could not comprehend. He wondered if anything he had ever done had really been his own doing. Everything seemed to be an illusion, of one kind or another. But the central mystery, the only thing that he was able to care about at all, was: What was the Brotherhood of Assassins? Whose side were they on? What were they trying to do?

Finally, they reached a small, silvery ship hidden in a great jumble of huge boulders. Duntov opened the airlock door, and they all climbed inside.

As soon as the outer airlock door was shut behind them, before he had even unsuited, Duntov said, "Got to get out of here fast! Guard them while they unsuit, and get them to the Cocoons as soon as possible. I'll get us ready for immediate liftoff." Then he was gone into the interior of the ship and the three prisoners were alone with the ten silent Brotherhood agents as they unsuited.

After they had unsuited, three of the Brotherhood men, laseguns drawn, led them to a small cabin with eight Gee-Cocoons.

"In!" one of them ordered curtly. Johnson climbed into a Cocoon, and Khustov and Gorov into two others. Only when they were thoroughly secured in the stress filament packing did the Brotherhood men climb into their own Cocoons.

Then a klaxon sounded, and Johnson felt a weightless, floating sensation as the antigravs cut in.

And the ship lifted off to whatever strange destination awaited them.

The ship continued to accelerate, and Johnson was pushed gently back in his Cocoon, the nest of stress filaments cradling him and, strangely, relaxing him somewhat.

Perhaps it was just the forced inactivity, perhaps merely the passage of time, but bit by bit, he felt his shocked lethargy leaving him. The life he had lived, his ten years in the Democratic League, was ruined, over, done with. There was no going back; there was nothing to go back to.

Yet Boris Johnson felt a certain buoyancy, an interest in what the next moment might bring, creeping up on him. The Hegemonic Council had completely outwitted him, true, played him for an utter fool. But the Brotherhood of Assassins had made the Council look even more foolish—the Hegemony wasn't invincible, it wasn't invulnerable.

He glanced across the aisle at Vladimir Khustov, pale, slack-jawed, dull-eyed in his own Cocoon. The Hegemonic Coordinator had lost more today than he had—Khustov had had more to lose in the first place. Khustov had been top dog, and now he was nothing, a thing at the mercy of the incomprehensible Brotherhood. At least I had nothing more to lose than a conspiracy that was doomed to failure from the beginning, he thought.

He began to wonder if, in fact, he didn't owe the Brotherhood a certain debt of gratitude, if he hadn't known that the Democratic League was futile all along. Perhaps he had fought on simply because there was nothing else to do, no place to go.

And now the Brotherhood had freed him from his past. Perhaps Arkady had really been telling the truth—maybe they *were* both fighting for the same thing. If so, the Brotherhood was certainly better at it. They had lasted for centuries, they had infiltrated the League and used it as a pawn, and they had at least one spaceship. . . . If the Brotherhood really was on the side of freedom, perhaps there would be a place for him in it. It was the fight for freedom, after all, that really counted, not who led it. And, Johnson was forced to admit, if the Brotherhood really was fighting for freedom, whoever was running it certainly seemed to know his business better than he did. . . .

Boris Johnson felt like a slate, wiped clean and waiting for fate to write upon it what it would. It was not an altogether unpleasant feeling. It was, in fact, that for which he had fought, the rarest of all feelings in the Hegemony of Sol—freedom.

Now the ship seemed to be changing course, and a large viewscreen came to life in the front of the cabin. Mercury, a yin-yang sphere of dead black and gristly brightness filled most of it, but Johnson could just make out two motes rising from the dayside, near where the environment dome was located.

"We're being followed," the voice of Arkady Duntov said over the ship's intercom. "Two heavy cruisers."

Vladimir Khustov's face suddenly came alive. He smiled smugly. "You cannot hope to escape two cruisers," he said. "Why not save yourself some trouble and surrender to me now? I promise that I will see to it that things go easier with you. Frankly, it would place me in a better position with the Council if you surrendered to me than if I had to be rescued. Give me that advantage, and I'll repay you when I'm restored to the Coordinatorship."

Duntov, unseen, laughed. "The Hegemony hasn't exactly encouraged scientific development," he said. "You lost your best spaceship designer quite a while ago, Dr. Richard Schneeweiss. The Brotherhood . . . acquired his services. This ship has certain modifications that should allow us to counter the cruisers' superior speed and firepower. Besides, if I were you, Khustov, I'd be rooting for us to escape. I somehow doubt that those ships have orders to capture us alive."

"I fear he's right, at least about the orders that Jack Torrence has issued," Gorov said. "We both know his ambitions, Vladimir. He has every reason and every excuse to order this ship destroyed on sight. With you dead, he'd be certain to permanently secure his position as Coordinator. I just hope our captors are as right about their ability to escape as they are about what goes on in Torrence's mind."

Johnson grinned as he saw the play of emotions on Khustov's troubled face. Khustov knew Torrence all too well, and now he was forced into hoping that his captors could elude his would-be "rescuers!"

The scene on the viewscreen changed: the screen grew very dark, and even the stars seemed to fade. . . . Then, as a great fiery globe came into view, Johnson saw why. The camera filter had been polarized to near opacity as the ship came around and headed inward, straight toward the fearful ball of raging plasma that was the sun.

The sun grew ever larger in the viewscreen. Sunspots like great spots of black mold became visible as the ship swept inward from Mercury's orbit.

"We'll be incinerated!" Johnson finally shouted. "We can't survive much closer to the sun!"

"Exactly what the commanders of those cruisers will think," Duntov said over the intercom. "But this ship has a new heat shield that Schneeweiss developed. It's like some kind of thermocouple device. The entire outer hull is a superefficient solar energy converter. It powers a pumping and cooling system that circulates liquid helium through a capillary system in the inner skin of the hull—and the hotter it gets outside, the more efficient the system becomes. Real neat—it uses the heat of the sun to cool the ship."

The sun grew larger and larger; now it filled almost the entire screen. Johnson had never heard of a ship approaching this close to the sun. Yet the interior temperature stayed comfortable. The cooling system, however it worked, was certainly doing the job.

"I think they've spotted us," Duntov said. "But it won't do them very much good. We're between them and the sun. This close in, radar won't work, their laser-rangers will be whited out and visual tracking is impossible."

"You can't stay in here forever, you fool!" Khustov said. "As soon as we turn around, they'll spot us. They've got us trapped up against the sun."

"Then we'll just have to vanish, eh?" Duntov replied.

The ship continued to drop toward the sun. A great solar prominence fountained from the sun several million miles to the left of the ship, a monstrous gout of plasma that reached beyond the ship's trajectory. Lord, we're close! Johnson thought as the viewscreen fuzzed from solar static. Down, down, down, toward the awesome solar furnace the ship sped. . . .

Then the bloated disc of the sun stopped growing—but it did not wane. Johnson could still feel the ship accelerating, yet they were neither approaching nor retreating from the sun now. . . .

All at once, Johnson realized what Duntov was doing. He was putting the ship into a cometary parabolic trajectory around the sun, using the ship's drive and the sun's enormous gravity to whip it around the sun like a stone on a string, putting the sun itself between the ship and its pursuers.

Johnson's guess was confirmed a moment later as the ship's rate of acceleration increased, continued to increase, as the sun caught it and whipped it around its equator, very much like a comet. . . . The ship maintained its distance from the sun as it continued to accelerate. They were in the proper parabolic orbit, and this close in, the sun was a double ally: it made it impossible for the cruisers to track them, and the sun's gravity added to their velocity as it whipped them, comet-wise, around it to the far side. They would indeed vanish! The Hegemonic commanders, not knowing about the new heat shield, would assume that they had risked coming too close to the sun and had been vaporized when they failed to detect the ship turning around and trying to sneak past them. They would not be likely to suspect that the ship had in fact swung around Sol—since that was a maneuver of which their own ships were incapable, and the Hegemony was utterly confident that its equipment was the best available.

And yes, now the sun was offset from the center of the screen as open space appeared to the left of it. They had begun to swing around it . . .

The sun became a half-disc, then a fat crescent on the right side of the viewscreen, then a thinner crescent that grew even smaller. . . . They were around it now, it was all but behind them. . . .

And now it *was* behind them as the thin crescent line on the right edge of the screen disappeared, and the polarization of the camera filter was decreased . . . and the stars came out.

"Home free!" Duntov said. "Next stop—Brotherhood headquarters!"

Despite the repugnancy of the situation, Constantine Gorov found himself trying to engage the Brotherhood agents in conversation—as much out of boredom as curiosity.

Wherever they were going, it was a long trip, and Khustov's conversation consisted mainly of grunts. Boris Johnson was quite willing to babble on—and did so at every opportunity—but the man was a fool, and Gorov knew as much about the Democratic League as he cared to, and then some.

But the Brotherhood of Assassins was quite another matter. These Brotherhood agents either had a very exaggerated sense of secrecy, or they were all totally ignorant. He had tried to open them up by quoting Markowitz' *Theory of*

Social Entropy, and even some of the man's more obscure works, such as *Culture and Chaos*, but all he had gotten for his pains were blank stares. Could it really be that these men were ignorant of the doctrine which they served? Most curious . . . it had a certain parallel with the Millennium of Religion. Then too, there had been believers who fought on the sides of the various dogmas, not because they were convinced of their accuracy, but simply because they Believed— without having any really sophisticated knowledge of exactly *what* it was that they believed in. A curious mental style indeed!

Perhaps this leader of theirs . . . Gorov thought as Duntov entered the cabin, stood idly in the front of the room. Gorov got out of his Cocoon and walked over to Duntov.

"You seem like a reasonably intelligent individual," Gorov began earnestly. "How can you really believe that the theories of Markowitz will actually enable you to overthrow the Hegemony? I must grant that his theories have a certain internal consistency, but it seems to me that the factor which invalidates them empirically is time. Markowitz never mentions time limitation in his discussion of the Order-Chaos paradoxes. That is, while I must concede that given infinite time, any ordered society must be destroyed by the spiraling paradoxes, it seems that Markowitz ignores the fact that the evolutionary span of the human race is itself finite. Or do you have access to additional works we don't know about?"

Gorov saw that the Brotherhood leader was staring at him utterly bewildered. "I . . . uh . . . haven't read much of Markowitz," Duntov said. "I really don't know what you're talking about."

Incredible! Gorov thought. Simply incredible! Even the leader is an utter ignoramus!

"You mean to tell me that you've given up all the advantages of a loyal Ward of the Hegemony without even knowing what you've given them up *for*?" Gorov exclaimed.

Duntov squirmed. "It's . . . it's just that there's something missing in the Hegemony," he said. "I've felt it as long as I can remember. The Brotherhood seems to have what's missing—we call it Chaos. I can believe in Chaos, and that makes me . . . makes me . . . makes me feel, well, *taken care of.*"

"And just what is this Chaos that gives you such a sense of security?"

Duntov shrugged. "Something much too big and powerful and eternal for me or any other man to really know," he said. "Something greater than Man, a force which rules the universe. . . . Surely, even you have felt the need to know that there was something, somewhere, greater than the human race. . . ?"

Fantastic! Gorov thought. Of course the man doesn't realize it, but he's talking about the concept the ancients called "God." An arcane new thought tickled Gorov's mind. Although all knowledge of the God-thesis had perished with the Millennium of Religion, was it possible that there existed in certain men an inborn need for this thing, a desire to discover and believe in some supernatural order or being, a desire that had no specific object, that was, in a sense, its *own* object?

An interesting theory indeed! he thought. Perhaps . . . perhaps if I survive all this, it will not be a total loss. Knowledge truly may be gained in the most unlikely places!

"Into your Cocoons, gentlemen," the voice of Arkady Duntov said over the intercom. "Touchdown in five minutes."

Johnson climbed into his Cocoon as the cabin viewscreen came on, showing a tiny, barren, seemingly uninhabited rock floating in empty space. The stress filaments enveloped him, but the antigravs did not cut in—the natural gravitic attraction of such a pebble would be nil, and any internal artificial gravity would not affect a body approaching it.

He saw that the ship was approaching the asteroid rapidly, as if Duntov were quite familiar with it, arcing toward it, and around to the far side in a fast, low trajectory. But there seemed to be nothing at all on the little planetoid—hardly a level spot on which to land. It was mostly jagged peaks and deep crevices—a huge drifting boulder.

Then, as the ship rounded the asteroid and started to decelerate, one of the jagged cracks that marked the asteroid's surface suddenly began to enlarge, almost like a clamshell opening, and Johnson saw that what he had taken for a natural rift in the surface was really part of a cleverly designed and camouflaged entrance portal—two huge sliding slabs, one on either side of the crack, covered with rock and opening smoothly to reveal a great pit dug into the surface of the asteroid itself at the bottom of which he could make out a metal-floored landing area . . . and a large one at that.

As the ship lowered itself into the concealed landing pit, Johnson saw that there were five similar ships sitting on the left half of the landing pad.

But the ship that occupied the right half of the pit was really a monster. It was huge, the biggest ship he had ever seen, bigger than anything the Hegemony had, as far as he knew. And the design was unlike anything he had ever heard of—a smooth, silvery hull with no visible drive, an elongated egg pointed at both ends with two broad bands of intricate-looking metalwork encircling the hull about its middle.

Even before the ship had touched down, the great doors were already sliding back into place above it, concealing the landing pit from any ship that might happen by, restoring the illusion of a completely uninhabited asteroid.

"What is that thing?" Johnson shouted at the intercom as he felt the ship touch down.

"The *Prometheus*," Duntov said. "The future of humanity. . . . And someday I'll be on it, and we'll go where there is no Hegemony to—"

"The Hegemony is everywhere!" Khustov shouted. "You *can't* escape from it!"

"Perhaps," Duntov said quickly, as if covering up some unguessable slip. "All I know is what I'm told—and I've been told to tell you no more. You'll know soon enough . . . those of you who Robert Ching means to let know. Now get out of your Cocoons, all of you. You're going to meet the most . . . the wisest man I've ever met."

But Boris Johnson was not thinking of the enigmatic Robert Ching, in whom Duntov seemed to place such blind trust, as he climbed out of the Cocoon.

Where there is no Hegemony . . . he thought. How can any ship go where there is no Hegemony? The Hegemony extends from Mercury to Pluto! Unless . . . unless . . . but everyone claimed that that was impossible! Everyone knew why it was impossible. . . .

Or did the Hegemony just want people to believe that it was impossible?

"Order, being anti-entropic, requires a fixed and limited context within which to exist. Chaos contains all such limited contexts within it as insignificant eddies temporarily resisting the basic universal tendency towards increased Social Entropy."

Gregor Markowitz,
The Theory of Social Entropy

11

Robert Ching sat alone at the great rock table in the meeting chamber. This day, this moment was to be a pinnacle in his life, in his career as First Agent—and there was no duality between his life and his career—and it was to be shared with no man.

Three men . . . Ching thought, all of them fearing imminent death at the hands of something they could not fathom. Yet none of them will die, unless by their own highly unlikely choice. Salvation for two of them and something perhaps worse than death for the third—certainly more Chaotic than simple extinction, at any rate.

Yes, all was falling rapidly into place like a centuries-long drama building to a climax. The *Prometheus* would be ready for its voyage in not too many more weeks. And Random Factors were proliferating in the Hegemony at the greatest rate in history. . . .

The League, the "Disloyal Opposition," was destroyed. Now, whenever anything untoward occurred, the Hegemonic Council would have to admit to itself—perhaps even to the Wards, if Brotherhood action took a more public and dramatic turn—that it was the work of the Brotherhood of Assassins, a force unknown, unpredictable, acting toward unguessable ends, not the work of an adolescent conspiracy like the League which could be readily comprehended and dealt with.

And the change on the Hegemonic Council itself would also lead to increased Social Entropy, Ching thought. Jack Torrence, opportunist that he is, will be far more flexible than Khustov—though even more ruthless. When the *Prometheus* at last opened the closed system of the Hegemony to infinite Chaos, Torrence, unlike Khustov, would try to use the new conditions to his own advantage rather than make the futile attempt to suppress the inevitable. An opportunist, even a near-psychopath like Torrence, was a much better type to have in power during a great social upheaval than a fanatic . . . Especially when the fanatic, partially discredited, was still around to keep him off balance. Yes, a live Vladimir Khustov could, in his way, serve Chaos. . . .

The intercom buzzer interrupted Ching's revery. He turned the audio on. "Yes?"

"The prisoners are outside, First Agent."

"Send them in," Robert Ching said. "And send them in alone. But have guards waiting outside in case of trouble."

A moment later, the chamber door opened, and Johnson, Gorov and Khustov were half-shoved inside by burly Brothers. Robert Ching studied their faces as the three men stood uncertainly before the table.

Boris Johnson seemed confused, skeptical perhaps, but not overly hostile. He seemed to be looking things over as if hoping to discover a new world, a world that might replace the one he had so suddenly lost. He had been stripped of all his illusions, Ching saw, and was hungry for new ones. A promising, if not entirely admirable attitude. . . .

The face of Vladimir Khustov was an open book. He was clearly terrified, but there was hate in his eyes too, and something akin to disgust—the loathing one fanatic feels for what he imagines to be another fanatic serving an alien creed. And perhaps, Ching half-conceded to himself, perhaps there is an element of truth in what his instincts tell him. . . .

Gorov, on the other hand, was quite unreadable. His

face was a bland, self-contained, emotionless mask. His reputation as a human robot, a creature motivated only by the lust for knowledge, a thinking machine, seemed to be well-justified. Yet, though Ching found Gorov quite repellent, he also felt a curious affinity to the man. Though they differed in all else, they both had a respect for the wonders of the universe around them that, though Gorov would certainly never admit it, bordered on the mystical. And of the three, Ching knew that Gorov would most easily understand what he was about to tell them.

"Welcome to the headquarters of the Brotherhood of Assassins," Ching said. "Please be seated, gentlemen."

Boris Johnson immediately seated himself at the far end of the table from Ching and stared at the First Agent with a naked curiosity that Robert Ching found quite engaging. The Johnsons, he realized, were by and large the best type that the human race could produce under the conditions of the Hegemony—instinctive rebels, viscerally dogmatic in their unthinking opposition to the Order of the Hegemony, but uncommitted and curiously flexible when it came to final ends.

Gorov hesitated for a moment, then sat down beside Johnson. Vladimir Khustov, however, made no move to seat himself, glared defiantly at Ching.

"Come, come, Mr. Khustov," Ching chided. "Surely you will not force me to summon guards to place you in your seat. It makes me uneasy to have you standing there like that, and I insist that you seat yourself. Don't make me use force. I abhor pointless violence."

"You . . . you . . ." Khustov stammered, sinking at last into a chair. "You abhor violence! You! The Brotherhood of Assassins! Murderers! Madmen! Insane fanatic killers! *You* abhor violence!"

"I said I abhor *pointless* violence," Robert Ching said mildly. "But the conditions of the Hegemony force violence upon even the most reasonable of men. Only through violence may the Hegemony be destroyed."

"Then Arkady was telling the truth?" Boris Johnson

exclaimed. "You *are* enemies of the Hegemony? But . . . but why've you opposed us at every turn? Surely you must know that the Democratic League is an enemy of the Hegemony! We could've cooperated. . . ." Johnson said almost wistfully. "We're the enemy of your enemy, if nothing else. Why have you fouled us up all along?"

How to explain to a man like Johnson that he has served that which he opposes by his very opposition? Ching thought. How to explain it without breaking him?

"You are familiar with the Law of Social Entropy?" Ching asked tentatively.

Johnson stared at him blankly.

Ching sighed. No, of course not! he thought. "You have heard of Gregor Markowitz, at least?"

"The prophet from the Millennium of Religion. . . ?" Johnson said. "The rumor is that you're his followers. Is it true that you base your decisions on reading the entrails of animals according to something called the 'Bible'? Is that why nothing you do makes sense?"

Ching laughed. "The entrails of animals!" he exclaimed. "The Bible! My friend, the Hegemony has kept you in ignorance more abysmal than I had ever imagined. We are not sorcerers and Markowitz was not a prophet as you think of it. He was what was once called a 'Social Scientist,' a man who studied human societies. *The Theory of Social Entropy* is not a book of prophecy, but a scientific treatise. I assure you, we are utterly logical in our actions. Our actions only appear illogical because they are Random."

"The two words mean the same thing," Johnson insisted.

"Yes, that is what the Hegemony would have you believe," Robert Ching said. "Order is logical, Chaos illogical. Those who serve Order are pragmatists and those who serve Chaos religious fanatics. But consider the Law of Social Entropy. Let me state it in terms you can understand. The natural tendency in the physical realm is toward ever-increasing randomness or disorder, what we call Chaos or entropy. So too, in the realm of human culture. To locally and temporarily reverse the trend towards entropy in the physical realm requires energy. And so too in human societies—Social Energy. The more Ordered, thus unnatural, anti-entropic, a society, the more Social Entropy is required to maintain the unnatural condition. And how is this Social Energy to be obtained? Why, by so ordering the society as to produce it! Which, as you can see, requires more Order in return. Which creates a demand for more Social Energy, and so forth, in a geometric progression that spirals as long as the society attempts to achieve Order. You see the paradox, do you not? The more Ordered a society becomes, the more Ordered it must become to maintain its original Order, requiring still more Social Energy, and never really catching up. Thus a society can tolerate less and less randomness as it grows ever more Ordered."

Ching saw that Johnson was struggling with the concept, his face knotted in perplexity.

"Think of it in specific terms," Ching suggested. "The Hegemony is a highly Ordered and unnatural structure, opposed to the basic Chaotic nature of the universe. The approach of your Democratic League was to fight that Order in an Ordered manner—and since the Hegemony is far more Ordered than the League could ever be, you could never obtain the Social Energy needed to substitute your Order for the existing Order. In fact, the League, as the "Disloyal Opposition" absorbed much of the random hostility to the Hegemony and converted these Random Factors to predictable ones and thus actually contributed to the Order of the Hegemony. We, on the other hand, by acting randomly, by introducing intolerable Random Factors, are assured of eventual success, since Chaos, the nature of the universe itself, is, in a very real sense, on our side."

"How long do we have to listen to this nonsense?" Vladimir Khustov exclaimed. "Kill us and be done with it! Do you have to add boredom to murder?"

"*Kill you?*" Ching said, smiling. "Indeed, that would be the logical, predictable thing to do, would it not? You are the enemy—kill the enemy, eh? Certainly what you would do in my position. But you serve Order, and I am an agent of Chaos. Therefore, I do the Chaotic thing, and the Chaotic thing in this situation is to let you go."

Ching grinned wryly as he saw the expressions on the faces of Khustov and Johnson. Hope on Khustov's face, more than a little contempt, and a thousand plans. Confusion on Johnson's. Only Constantine Gorov's face was calm, seemed perhaps knowing. It had been a wise decision indeed, to remove Gorov from the Hegemonic Council. The man was brilliant and lusted almost obscurely for knowledge. Had that lust been combined with an equal lust for power. . . . Gorov in the Coordinatorship would've been a formidable opponent indeed!

"But of course," Ching continued, "you will be asked to tarry awhile as our guest at another Brotherhood base. Six standard months seems like a suitable period. After that, you will be released. The reaction of Jack Torrence to your sudden reappearance after a six month stay with the Brotherhood of Assassins should be most . . . Chaotic."

Khustov paled. "You can't do that!" he cried. "The Council will think that I've been aligned with the Brotherhood all along. Torrence has been filling their ears with that innuendo. They'll . . . they'll have me executed!"

"Perhaps," said Robert Ching. "Then again, perhaps not. Since we've given Torrence the Coordinatorship, I think it only fair that I supply you with a suggestion that may insure your survival. Consider: you might point out to the Council that the execution of a former Coordinator would not look good for the Hegemony—especially if it were implied that you had been an agent of the Brotherhood. It would imply that the Brotherhood had been able to infiltrate the Hegemonic Council itself. Moreover, even eliminating you from the Council would be a bad move for the same reason—it would raise questions in the minds of the Wards for which there would be no easy answers. A man of your talents should even be able to convince the Council to let you remain a Councilor until you came up for election again."

Ching pressed a button on his communicator. "Send in the guards to remove Mr. Khustov," he said.

A moment later, the door opened and five armed Brothers entered. Ching watched Khustov being conducted from the chamber with a feeling of deep satisfaction. Social Entropy had indeed been maximized. Khustov and Torrence, for the remaining years of Khustov's term on the Council, would exchange places, with Torrence as Coordinator and Khustov as a focus of opposition. And the Brotherhood, by suitable action, could even make it seem that Torrence was in league with it. Once again, a divided Council. And long before Khustov came up for election, the *Prometheus* would return from its mission, would return to confront a Hegemonic Council divided against itself. With the forces of Order deeply divided, and the forces of Chaos backed up by the proof that the Galaxy was a great, infinite concourse of civilizations, a knowledge too vast, too revolutionary to long deny or suppress. . . . The Hegemony of Sol faced certain doom, and the centuries of holding actions, of introducing minor Random Factors into the closed system of the Hegemony would at last be vindicated. And Chaos would reign supreme forever!

When Khustov had been removed, Constantine Gorov spoke for the first time.

"So my supposition was correct all along," Gorov said. "The seemingly senseless acts of the Brotherhood really *were* the introduction of random factors into the Hegemonic Order in line with the work of Markowitz. An interesting body of work, to be sure, but one with flaws, flaws which insure your eventual defeat."

"Ah yes, Gorov . . ." Ching said, somewhat amused. "No doubt a man of your intellect should be able to shoot all kinds of holes in a theory that has stood up for over three centuries."

"Quite so," Gorov said, totally humorlessly. "You see, the basic flaw in Markowitz' thinking is his very obsession with universality and infinity. In the abstract, I must grant that a closed system such as the Hegemony must eventually succumb to random factors as Order increases towards the absolute. In the long run—the *very* long run. But we are dealing with specifics, not abstractions. In the long run, the Hegemony is doomed—as are all the works of men, since the evolutionary span of the human race itself is finite. But time is the factor that works against you, time is what the Theory of Social Entropy so blandly ignores. Certainly, your strategy would work—if you had eternity in which to make it work. But you don't have anything like eternity. In the long run, Man, like every species before him, will become extinct, when the sun grows cold, and probably long before that, destroyed by factors at which we cannot even guess. And that extinction will occur long before you can bring down the Hegemony—for the Hegemony too plays for time, and soon the Hegemony will exercise total control over the entire Solar System, over the entire habitat of Man. It will be a perfect closed system. While it may be true that such a system will be able to tolerate ever fewer random factors, it is also true that it will be harder and harder to introduce such factors, and the Hegemony will be able to stave off its demise for millions of years—in fact for the entire span of existence of the human race. You're not the only ones capable of taking the long view—and therein lies the fatal flaw in your strategy."

Ching was stunned at Gorov's insight, for Gorov had put his finger squarely on that paradox which had darkened the minds of the best thinkers of the Brotherhood for centuries—until Project Prometheus had proved feasible. Ching was convinced more strongly than ever of the wisdom of removing such a man from the enemy camp—and the hope was strengthened in him that a creature with a mind like Gorov's, a creature so dominated by brilliant logic—might very well be won over to the side of Chaos by intellectual persuasion.

"You do not disappoint me, Constantine Gorov," Ching said. "You have given a perfect analysis of the dynamics of a closed social system. Markowitz himself would be impressed. Provided, of course, that the discussion, that the realm of Man, must always be confined to such a closed, finite system.

"But consider. . . . Consider the Galaxy, consider the

entire universe. The universe itself is infinite, hence is intrinsically an *open*, Chaotic system. In such a context, an Ordered mote such as the Hegemony cannot long endure."

"You cloud the issue!" Gorov insisted. "We're talking about pragmatic reality, not fantasy. We're talking about the finite habitat of Man, the Solar System, not hypothetical infinity."

"Ah," said Ching, "but *must* Man inevitably be confined to this solar system, doomed to extinction when Sol dies? Might not Man someday hatch, like a chicken from the closed egg it imagines to be the universe in its embryonic existence, into a far vaster realm. The realm of Chaos and infinity— and racial immortality?"

Ching stared at the now thoughtful faces of Gorov and Johnson.

"It is time, I think," he said, "to show you something that will shake your outlooks to the core, as it shook mine. . . . As it will shake the universal outlook of the entire human race."

He spoke into the communicator. "Prepare the probe-film for immediate viewing in the auditorium."

Boris Johnson followed Ching, Gorov and four guards out of the cavelike chamber, down a corridor to the mouth of a droptube in a fascinated daze. Something seemed to be probing at the limits of his consciousness—the answer to some question he could not quite formulate. Much of this "Theory of Social Entropy" and the exchange between Gorov and Ching had seemed incomprehensible, yet there was something about what Ching had said that seemed somehow *right,* more than right—obvious, self-evident. . . .

And as the tube's antigravs lowered him, along with the others, toward the center of the asteroid, it all suddenly seemed to come into focus. All his life, as long as he could remember, he had hated the Hegemony without really being sure why; had been determined to destroy it with no more than the vaguest notion as to how.

But now it had been revealed to him that other men

shared his feelings—men who, unlike himself, had access to
the forgotten, suppressed wisdom of the past, who understood the essential nature of that which they were fighting,
who knew how to fight it effectively, and, most important
of all, seemed to have a grander vision of human destiny
than merely the destruction of the Hegemony, who saw that
overthrow as no more than the prelude to something vast
and immortal.

And that, he knew, was what the Democratic League
had lacked. The League had merely been *against* something;
there was nothing that it had been for. Even "Democracy"
had been thought of as only the absence of the Hegemony—
the negation of a negative, not a positive vision in its own
right.

But the Brotherhood had this thing called Chaos—a concept hard to grasp, elusive, he suspected, not because it was
a mere word, but because of its very grandeur.

He stared at Robert Ching as they reached the bottom
of the droptube and the Brotherhood leader led them down
a corridor to a door in the rock wall, and he knew that he
was looking at a man who had a unifying vision of the universe, of everything around him. This Chaos that was somehow the very nature of existence itself had given Ching an
unerring insight into everyday reality—and the proof of that
was that the Brotherhood had been able to outwit both the
League and the Hegemony at every turn. Now he could begin
to understand Arkady Duntov's near-worship of Ching. It
was not every man who could fully comprehend Chaos, but
it was clear that Robert Ching did. If one could not understand it all oneself, there was at least something to be said
for uncritically following a man who did. . . .

Now Ching led them into a small auditorium with a screen
at the front and a projector, manned by a technician, at the
rear. Wordlessly, Ching motioned them to seats, took one
himself and, still without uttering a word, nodded to the
technician.

And the screen before them came to life.

Johnson saw a spangle of stars against a black background, one of them growing in what seemed discontinuous jumps, showing a disc, the disc waxing, becoming ever-larger, ever-closer. . . .

"What you're looking at," Ching said, "is part of the edited film taken by an unmanned interstellar probe."

Beside him, Johnson heard Gorov gasp. "Interstellar flight!" Gorov muttered. "A faster-than-light drive. . . ? Impossible! Only Schneeweiss himself was capable of . . . And he killed himself when those fools on the Council suppressed his work over my objections. . . . *Didn't he?*"

"What do *you* think?" Robert Ching said as the images of several assorted planets flickered across the screen, as one image finally replaced the rapid montage—the image of a green planet, a planet with oceans and white cloud cover . . . A planet orbiting another sun! Johnson suddenly fully realized, overcome by the wonder, the sheer fascination of it all.

Gorov was silent as the film continued to unreel. Ching too said no more as the screen began to reveal continents and vegetation and coastlines and cultivated fields. Johnson too was stone silent, hardly breathing. What was there that any man could say? He was seeing with his own eyes the most important event in human history, an event so enormous, so pregnant with infinite possibilities that it utterly staggered him. That men might someday go to the stars! A whole new solar system, eventually many new systems. . . . Here was a real hope for freedom, a hope based on solid objective fact, not mere wishful thinking!

And then he grunted aloud as the screen showed the alien city. Once more he gasped as the strange alien craft appeared in the field of vision.

Then the film was over and the screen went blank.

"Now you have seen it," Robert Ching said. "Now you know the most important fact in all of human history. Man is no longer alone. And the film you saw was taken on the 61 Cygnus system, a nearby system by Galactic standards, and the very first system we've probed. Consider: if we happened upon a highly developed alien civilization on our first try, how many such civilizations must exist in our Galaxy alone? Millions? Billions? And how many unoccupied but habitable planets? Where is your closed system now, Gorov? Can the Hegemony even dream of controlling an entire Galaxy?"

"No. . ." Gorov muttered. "Yes. . . I see that you are right, in this new context. The Hegemony is of course predicated upon the confinement of the human race to a limited area. But if men ever go to the stars, if the potential habitat of the race becomes infinite, obviously the Hegemony is doomed—and I would not mourn its passing, for it would no longer be a useful, functional, social construct. A great pity. . . ."

"In the light of what you've seen, you still mourn for the Hegemony, Gorov?" Ching said. "I expected better from a man of your intellect."

"You mistake my meaning," Gorov said. "My loyalty was never to the Hegemony as such—when conditions change, forms must change with them. The fools on the Hegemonic Council could never understand that. My loyalty is only to the truth, the truth and that social order which serves the best interests of the greatest possible number under any given conditions. Until now, that has been the peace and prosperity secured by the Order of the Hegemony. But when conditions change, a logical man reforms his hypotheses and analyses accordingly. If I mourn anything, I mourn the fact that the Hegemony will never permit interstellar travel. Surely you realize that they would know what it would mean. A great pity—such a vast store of new knowledge awaits us out there."

"Ah," said Ching, "but as you have seen, the Hegemony is not the only organization capable of building ships. Project Prometheus, the culmination of the three hundred year history of the Brotherhood of Assassins, is very near completion. And Project Prometheus is—"

"*A starship!*" Boris Johnson suddenly exclaimed. "That weird-looking ship we saw on the way in. It's a starship, isn't it?"

"Yes," said Robert Ching, "the *Prometheus* is indeed a starship. Within a month, it will depart for the 61 Cygnus system. And like its namesake, when it returns from its mission, for better or for worse, the course of human culture will be altered forever. The era of the Hegemony will come to an end. Consider: when the news becomes known—and rest assured, the Brotherhood will make it known—Torrence must decide either to build starships or to attempt to suppress interstellar travel. And for purely political reasons, if Torrence takes one side, Khustov must take the other. And there is something more that you do not know. Our probe was followed back by an alien probe. Clearly, the Cygnans will soon be capable of building starships of their own. Either man will go to the stars—or the stars will come to Man. In the end, it will come to the same thing: Man will inevitably be thrust forth into the Galaxy. And that will mean the end of the Hegemony. Control will give way to freedom, and Order to Chaos—and to infinity. And you, gentlemen, will be given the opportunity of participating directly in this greatest of all adventures."

Ching turned to face Johnson, and Johnson thought he saw something that was almost envy in Ching's calm brown eyes. "You, Boris Johnson," he said, "have earned a place on the *Prometheus*. Though you fought in ignorance, you fought on the side of Man, and such courage will be needed when we stand face to face with other sentient beings. Moreover, we must make it clear at the outset that the stars belong to all men, not just the Hegemony—or the Brotherhood of Assassins."

Ching faced Constantine Gorov. "And you," he said, "are ideally equipped to deal with non-humans. I confess that I don't find your coldness, your lack of human emotion, an endearing quality, but your lust for pure knowledge and your brilliance will serve Man well in comprehending a totally alien civilization, in bringing about true communication with a nonhuman culture."

Ching paused, smiled thinly. "But we believe in giving men at least a *pro forma* choice," he said. "Not much of a choice, I admit, but a choice nevertheless. You will willingly choose to go on the *Prometheus*, gentlemen, or you will be humanely executed. The choice, such as it is, is yours. What will it be, my friends?"

Johnson's head nodded, as much an involuntary movement as a gesture of assent. For he was quite staggered; he had been defeated, destroyed, his entire world cruelly exposed as a series of delusions—and now he was being offered a new life, one quite literally beyond his wildest dreams. For just as he had viscerally sensed the *rightness,* the self-evident quality of the Theory of Social Entropy without fully comprehending it, so too he instantly, instinctually realized that the opening of the Galaxy to the human race, the freedom of Man to roam a vast Galaxy inhabited by countless sentient races, was the epitome of all he had ever fought for, though he had never even recognized it as a possibility before.

His war on the Hegemony had been a fight for Democracy, which to him had simply meant freedom, and now he knew that the deepest meaning of freedom was not freedom *from* any particular tyranny or indeed from tyranny itself, but freedom *to*. And for men to be truly free, that "to" had to be open-ended, had to refer to every possibility that could ever exist. Freedom was the right of every man to fulfill his own private destiny, and there were at least as many destinies as there were men. Freedom was infinity. And only the stars were a concrete form of this theoretical freedom. In an infinite universe, Man would have the room to become infinite himself, and, being infinite, perhaps immortal. And he himself, personally, beyond the Hegemony at last, would at last be able to breathe free—not in some distant dream, but right here, right now!

Boris Johnson knew that he had caught a glimpse of the true, oceanic, pregnant nature of the universe, where all things were possible and all things that were possible *were* that infinite nature of existence that Robert Ching called Chaos.

He nodded his head again, willfully, firmly, this time. "I'll go," he said. "I'll go gladly."

"And you, Constantine Gorov?" said Robert Ching.

"You insult me," Gorov said humorlessly. "You insult

me by threatening me with death if I do not agree to accept the greatest challenge to my intellect that I could ever conceive of. Do you take me for an utter, blind fool? What sane man would refuse to accept such an opportunity? The extent of the knowledge to be gained by contact with a totally alien civilization is quite literally inconceivable, since such creatures must inevitably differ from ourselves in ways we cannot even imagine, must have formed thoughts that have never taken shape in human brains. It will be very much like emerging naked into our own civilization. We will gain millennia of new knowledge all but instantly! An unthinkable treasure. Of course I accept! What madness it would be to choose death over such knowledge!"

"I had thought that perhaps your loyalty to the Hegemony—"

"But the Hegemony is but a transient thing," Gorov said. "A structure which I still contend has served Man well in a given context. But now the context expands, and we must expand with it. For knowledge, once gained, cannot be thrown away, even if one were mad enough to want to. Knowledge alone is immutable and immortal."

"You have chosen well, gentlemen," Robert Ching said. "My only regret is that I cannot go with you. But adventure is not for the old, and there will be many things to do here. The work of the Brotherhood will not be ended until all mankind is free to join you in voyaging to the stars. The *Prometheus* is only a beginning. Like its namesake, it will bring the fire of the gods—Chaos, infinity—to Man. But men must make of that gift something good, not evil. There will be work here for the Brotherhood as long as there is a Hegemony. . . . But I'm woolgathering, and there is no time for that. We have a great deal of work to do in the next month, gentlemen. Let us begin."

> *"Man reaches for life and shrinks from death;*
> *Man reaches for Victory and shrinks from*
> *defeat. Therefore, what greater paradox than*
> *triumph through death? What act can be more*
> *truly Chaotic than victory through suicide?"*
>
> Gregor Markowitz,
> Chaos and Culture

12

Arkady Duntov stood in the control room of the *Prometheus*, in the control room of what he had gradually come to think of as *his* ship during this final month of preparation, the month that would at last end tomorrow.

For, at least while on the way to the 61 Cygnus system, it would indeed be his ship. He was the captain, the titular-leader of the expedition. Once they reached their goal, other men, even Gorov, a former enemy, would become more important, but coming and going, it was *his* ship.

And tomorrow, the day would come at last. The last of the supplies were being loaded, and tomorrow the full crew would come aboard and they would be on their way. Duntov ran his eyes lovingly over the now familiar controls and viewscreens.

There were really two independent control systems, one quite familiar, the other unlike that on any other ship. Each controlled one of the *Prometheus'* two drive systems. For lifting-off, making planetfalls and traveling within the limits of solar systems, the ship had quite conventional antigravs and reaction drive. Only when they had crossed the orbit of Pluto could the other propulsion system, the faster than light drive, be used.

Duntov shook his head for what seemed to him like the thousandth time as he scanned the FTL controls. In the past month, he had had endless sessions with Schneeweiss; yet, while the operation of the drive was simple enough, the theory was still all but incomprehensible to him.

"The *Prometheus* will not actually contradict the Einsteinian equations which limit the speed of all bodies to that of light," he remembered Schneeweiss as saying—and then taking over half an hour to explain just what those equations that he had not contradicted were. "So . . . you see," Schneeweiss had explained, after pointing out that according to those equations, it would take a transfinite force to accelerate a ship beyond the speed of light in what he called the 'prime continuum,' "we cannot exceed the speed of light in terms of the ship's passage through the prime space time continuum. Therefore, we escape from the prime continuum. You use the conventional drive to set a course for 61 Cygnus and to build up a large conventional velocity. Then you activate the Stasis-Generator. The *Prometheus*, with a small volume of space surrounding it, is then enclosed in a bubble of time, or more accurately, a field in which time stops, relative to the prime continuum. Relative to the microcontinuum within the field, the ship does not exceed the speed of light, but the bubble itself moves through the prime continuum at the speed of light raised to its own power. Since the ship will have ceased to occupy a space time locus in the prime continuum, the Einsteinian equations are not violated."

It had all been about as comprehensible as Markowitz' *Theory of Social Entropy*, which Robert Ching had given him to read—which was to say that Duntov understood most of the words, without really being quite able to grasp the concepts they described.

But in both cases, the elusiveness of the concepts did not really trouble him. He knew enough to act, to carry out his orders and pilot the ship, and that was all he really had to know—perhaps all he really wanted to know. Let other men play with their theories, he thought.

For Arkady Duntov knew his own limitations and his place in the scheme of things and he was content with both. There would always be things in the universe that he could never understand, things he did not really yearn to understand. It was quite enough to know that there were men who did understand them, men, like Robert Ching, in whom he could place unquestioning, but not entirely blind trust. He did not envy Ching or Gorov or Schneeweiss their knowledge. The demand to know was foreign to him. It was important only to believe, and to be able to act upon that belief.

And both had been granted to him. He would play an important part, an active part, in the great events to come. He was content with that and envied no man.

And as he thought back over the weeks of preparation, he wondered if men who knew and, like Robert Ching, could not act for one reason or another, did not perhaps, in some hidden recesses of their minds, envy him. . . .

Constantine Gorov floated beside Robert Ching in the great globular observation room in the core of the asteroid, the illusion of space and stars engulfing him, surrounding him, and bringing with it a curious kind of vertigo that, like Robert Ching himself, both repelled and fascinated him. He had been drawn to this place often in his month at Brotherhood headquarters—as he had been drawn to the company of Robert Ching.

Ching, he thought, is a most peculiar man. In so many ways, much like myself—a man who respects knowledge, a man with a real mind, and a man who respects others for respecting knowledge, an attitude all too rare in the human race.

Yet there was another side of Ching that Gorov found quite repulsive. How could such an intelligent man have such a backward, superstitious attitude toward the knowledge he acquired? This Chaos obsession of his. . . . It was a religion with the man, no doubt about it. There was something quite ludicrous—yet also somehow frightening—about a man of Ching's obvious intellect worshipping void, worshipping ran-

domness, worshipping, one might almost be tempted to say, the Heisenberg Uncertainty Principle. . . .

"Look at it, Gorov," Ching was saying. "All those stars, each a sun, each a possible habitat for Man . . . the utter infinity of Chaos, the sheer size of the universe. . . ."

But suddenly Gorov was not listening. He had spotted something, a tiny formation of specks moving towards them from sunward, from the direction of Earth. . . .

"Look!" he shouted, pointing. "Over there! Ships!"

Ching started, then followed Gorov's pointing hand. "Tracking command!" he spoke into the empty air. "Ships approaching the asteroid! Can you identify them? Compute their trajectory immediately!"

There was a long, long pause, during which cold resignation alternated with deep despair in Gorov's mind. Whose ships could they be but the Hegemony's? he thought. How could anyone hope to stop them? To be deprived of the chance to go to the stars now, at the last moment, with so much knowledge waiting. . . .

Then the voice of the tracking officer filled the observation room: "They're Hegemonic cruisers, First Agent. Thirty of 'em. They're headed straight for us, as if they know we're here. Estimated time of arrival—three standard hours."

"Impossible!" exclaimed Robert Ching. "All our installations are hidden. We've been maintaining absolute radio silence. Even our reactor is so heavily shielded that no one could possibly detect us by radiation emission. How. . . ?"

"Sheer Hegemonic thoroughness," Gorov said. "Torrence must've guessed that the Brotherhood headquarters would have to be somewhere in the Belt. After that . . . well, he's had a month to investigate. There's one thing you can't hide completely—*heat*. They've probably gone over every asteroid in the Belt with supersensitive heat detectors. A tedious task, admittedly. But none of the asteroids have internal heat-sources. Therefore, any asteroid that shows a temperature-differential with the space surrounding it obviously has to be inhabited. There was nothing you could've done to mask it. Those cruisers . . . you can't stand against them. But we have three hours . . . couldn't we load the *Prometheus* in time and lift off?"

"We could," said Ching, "but the *Prometheus* could never outrun the cruisers. It's somewhat slower than an ordinary ship in conventional drive, and it would be destroyed if the Stasis-Generator were activated this close to a stellar mass, or so Schneeweiss says. There's nothing we can do. Unless . . . unless . . ."

The expression on Ching's face slowly changed from one of total despair to what seemed to Gorov to be a look of triumph, almost of ecstasy. "Of course!" Ching exclaimed. "An Ultimate Chaotic Act! It's the only way! The Ultimate Chaotic Act, and fully justified by the circumstances, too! What could be more fitting?"

He turned to Gorov, and now Gorov could all but feel the mad glow the man seemed to be giving off, an unmistakable aura of religious ecstasy that thoroughly repelled and frightened him and yet filled him with a foolish, groundless hope, a hope that made him ashamed of his own illogicality. What was this brilliant fanatic thinking of? There was no way out. And what was an "Ultimate Chaotic Act?"

"Hurry!" Ching said. "To the *Prometheus*! Get all your things aboard. Man will have the stars, and I . . . I will be allowed an Ultimate Chaotic Act."

Gorov paused, was about to ask just what an "Ultimate Chaotic Act" was. But when he looked into Ching's eyes, into his deep, glowing eyes, which seemed to be fixed upon some far and terrible vision, Constantine Gorov was quite surprised to learn that he had at last encountered something he did not wish to know.

Boris Johnson, after more than two hours of dashing frantically about—helping with the last minute emergency loading, stowing his own gear, and what seemed to him like a thousand other hurried little tasks—now found himself at last swathed in stress-fibers in a Gee-Cocoon in the control room of the *Prometheus*. Beside him, in the special pilot's Cocoon which left his hands free, Arkady Duntov was running through last minute checkouts, speeding through the accelerated countdown. The other three Cocoons in the control room were occupied by men he hardly knew while Gorov and a hundred other men were cradled like eggs packed for shipment beyond the rear bulkhead of the control room in the main cabins of the ship. All was about ready for liftoff.

But now, with nothing left to do but wait, with the flurry of feverish activity behind him, Johnson realized how futile all the rushing around had been, how hopeless their position was.

Hegemonic cruisers were less than half an hour away, and the way they were making for the asteroid at top speed made it perfectly clear that they knew exactly where they were going and why. The *Prometheus* could not hope to outrun them this side of Pluto, and all the small Brotherhood ships on the asteroid could not buy them five minutes' time against thirty cruisers.

It was hopeless . . . and yet Johnson had experienced hopelessness too many times in the past few months without actually succumbing to be able to feel that any seemingly hopeless situation was utterly final.

And the whole Brotherhood base had seemed to be busy in a flurry of what had at least seemed like meaningful activity. They were planning *something*, and several times he had overheard Prime Agents murmuring about something called the "Ultimate Chaotic Act," with peculiar tense-yet-ecstatic looks on their faces. It was clear that there were those who knew something he didn't—a situation that Johnson had come more and more to accept as normal, lately. But what could that something be. . . ?

The center screen in the big bank of viewscreens in front of Duntov came on, and Johnson saw the big, tight formation of silvery, graceful yet somehow sinister Hegemonic ships making for the asteroid.

And then the voice of Robert Ching came over the communicator: "Agent Duntov, you will not answer me. You will maintain absolute radio silence from here on in. You will obey orders exactly." Ching's voice sounded uncharacteristically tense, and there was a steely new note in it; the note of command.

"Your orders are as follows," Ching continued. "You will hold the *Prometheus* in readiness for immediate liftoff, but you will not lift off until the signal is given. The signal will be the opening of the doors above the landing pit. The moment the doors open, you will lift off. You will not pause to correct your course for 61 Cygnus at this time. You will head in the general direction of 61 Cygnus, maintaining full emergency acceleration until the danger of interception by Hegemonic ships is clearly past. Do not worry—you'll know when that time comes. Only then will you make your final course corrections. Obey these orders to the letter and serve Chaos well. Out—*and goodbye*."

"But what about the Hegemonic ships—" Duntov started to say into the communicator, then, apparently remembering Ching's order to maintain radio silence, redirected the question, rhetorically, at Johnson. "We can't outrun them, Boris. And they can't outgun them with the ships they have here. And the nearest Brotherhood base is days away . . ."

"Don't ask *me*, Arkady," Johnson said. "This is the Brotherhood's show. But Ching seems to know what he's doing. He's always come out on top before."

"Yes . . ." Duntov murmured. "Robert Ching won't fail us."

I wish I had your blind faith, Arkady . . . Johnson thought bleakly. Or *do* I. . . ?

The great observation room in the center of the honey-combed asteroid was packed with Brothers—Prime Agents, field agents, technicians—every man on the asteroid who was not on the *Prometheus* floated somberly in the gravityless pseudo-space, ominously quiet and still.

The only clear area was near one quadrant of the globular viewscreen-wall that enclosed the chamber, where Robert Ching floated, back to the viewscreen wall, facing a series of devices which hung weightless in the air before him with cables leading from them through the solemn throng and up the open end of the droptube which sat like a hole in space itself high above him: a small control box with two toggle switches, two viewscreens, and a radio transceiver.

One viewscreen showed the false rock covering of the doors above the landing pit; the other a superficially-similar stretch of barren, comparatively flat, rocky plain on the other side of the asteroid.

Ching turned from the viewscreens jury-rigged before him and faced the far vaster panorama of stars and space that curved behind, above, and below him, surrounding him with the majesty of infinite space—a majesty now marred by the formation of Hegemonic ships that he could see making orbit around the asteroid, swinging now above him, now behind, below, and in front again, circling like wolves closing in for the kill.

Ching stared longingly at the stars, at the stars he would never see, at the wonders the *Prometheus* would probe, the wonders he would never know of now. . . .

But death, he thought, is the one moment every man must sooner or later face. It cannot be avoided, at best one can only hope to die a death filled with meaning. And how many men had ever been fortunate enough to choose the most meaningful death of all—the Ultimate Chaotic Act, Victory through suicide, paradox of paradoxes. What more fitting end to a lifetime in the service of Chaos. . . ?

But now, he thought, tearing himself away from the jewels on velvet panorama and returning to his instruments, now I must act. There will be moments for final reflection and contemplation later.

He activated the radio transceiver, feeling the tension of the men crowding the chamber mount as the first act of this final drama began.

"Brotherhood base to Hegemonic flotilla commander . . ." Ching said as the formation of ships spiraled ever closer to the surface of the asteroid. "Brotherhood base to Hegemonic flotilla commander. . . ."

A crisp, harsh voice answered over the transceiver: "This

is Vice-Admiral Lazar, Commander, Hegemonic Flotilla Thirty-four, speaking. Your asteroid base has been cordoned off. We have sufficient firepower to vaporize the entire asteroid. You will not attempt to escape. You will not attempt resistance. Half of my force will land and the other half will stand by ready to destroy you should you be so foolish as to attempt to resist capture. You will acknowledge immediately."

Ching's mind worked in an uncharacteristic frenzy. The Ultimate Chaotic Act he had planned required that *all* the Hegemonic ships land on the asteroid. They must all be destroyed if the *Prometheus* was to have a clear path to the edge of the Solar System and thence to the stars. If even one of the cruisers escaped, it would be able to overhaul the *Prometheus* and destroy it. . . . This Admiral must be made to land his entire force!

Robert Ching smiled a grim little smile. The way to make a man do what you want him to do, he thought, is to forbid him to do it.

"Brotherhood base to Vice-Admiral Lazar . . ." he said. "We realize that we have no hope of escape. However, there are several thousand well-armed Brothers on this base, and if we choose, we can make your victory a most costly one. But we are willing to negotiate a peaceful surrender in order to avoid pointless bloodshed. You will land your flagship alone and the rest of your ships will remain in orbit while we negotiate terms. Anything else will be met by resistance to the last man."

"You dare to dictate to me!" the Hegemonic Commander all-but-hissed in cold fury. "You think me imbecile enough to land alone on a base swarming with armed men? I will do the dictating here. I have thirty ships with a hundred armed assault troops on each. I fully intend to land *all* of them immediately, whether you like it or not. You may resist if you choose. See how far you get against three thousand Guards."

"Very well," Ching said, feigning tired resignation. "I

see we are outnumbered. We will not resist as long as your troops do not open fire on us. You may land on the sunward side of the asteroid."

"I will land *my* ships where *I* choose!" Lazar barked.

"Admittedly, the choice is yours," Ching said dryly. "However, to protect ourselves, I feel I must warn you that the far side of this asteroid is but a false face—nothing more than struts and a thin camouflage skin simulating rock and concealing our installations. Should you attempt to land *there*, your ships will crash onto our installations—killing all of us and yourself as well."

"Very well," Lazar said sullenly. "We'll land on the sunward side and our full troop compliment will proceed to your base overland. Remember, any resistance will result in your total annihilation. Out."

Robert Ching turned off the radio transceiver and raised his eyes from his instruments to gaze squarely upon the Brothers gathered in the globular chamber.

"The die is cast and there is no turning back now," he said gravely. "We have but minutes of life left as all of you know. The sequence is simple. All the Hegemonic ships will be allowed to land. Once they are all down, it would take them several minutes to lift off again. When they are all landed, I will throw the first switch"—he gestured toward the control box hanging weightless between himself and the assembled Brothers—"and the doors of the landing pit will open and the *Prometheus* will immediately lift off."

He paused, sighed, then continued. "It has been calculated that none of the Hegemonic ships will be able to lift off in less than three minutes from the moment they spot the *Prometheus*. Therefore, the *Prometheus* will be given two minutes and fifty seconds to clear the asteroid before the second switch is thrown. I don't have to tell you what *that* will mean. . . ."

Ching was silent for a long moment, and when he spoke again, it was as a man transfigured, speaking more to himself than to the Brothers, more to posterity, to Chaos, than to himself. A cold, chilling yet glacially calm ecstasy turned his features into the face of a totem, staring through the men and beyond and by its very Olympian indifference transforming them into willing acolytes.

"The Ultimate Chaotic Act," Robert Ching said with solemn ecstasy. "Victory through Suicide. Immortality through death. Never before in the history of the Brotherhood of Assassins has victory been within our grasp. Therefore never before has an Ultimate Chaotic Act been conceivable. We die willingly, with the greatest of honors, that Chaos may triumph, that Man may have the stars, and freedom, and immortality. But what is our deaths? All men die; few choose the moment of their death. Such a choice may be exercised by any man at any time—suicide is the one right that no tyranny can repress—but never before in our history could suicide bring victory. It has been given to all of us to share in an Ultimate Chaotic Act. No more fitting death is possible to a servant of Chaos. We die, as men do, but the Brotherhood lives on, as it always has. Men pass, but Chaos endures and those who serve it prevail through it. There will be no time for farewells later—so now, goodby. All of you have served Chaos well in life. Now you will give Chaos the ultimate service in death. Chaos, gentlemen—Chaos and victory!"

Not a man moved or spoke. Robert Ching was proud of his Brothers. They had been preparing for this moment since the Hegemonic flotilla had been spotted, he knew. But in a larger sense, they had been preparing for it all their lives. All that had to be said had been said. It remained but to act.

Ching turned his attention to the viewscreen which showed the sunward side of the asteroid, on the opposite side of the asteroid from the landing pit. Already, the rocky surface was growing a small forest of graceful, silvery ships. More ships came down, and Ching began to count them . . . fifteen . . . seventeen . . . twenty. . . .

Now outer airlock doors were opening on some of the

earlier arrivals, and the ships began to disgorge armed and spacesuited men onto the surface of the asteroid, even as more ships landed.

Twenty-three . . . twenty-seven . . . *thirty*! They were all down.

Ching's hand paused over the switch that would open the landing pit doors. Best to wait till all the ships had debarked men, in order to insure the maximum confusion when the *Prometheus* lifted off. . . .

Men continued to pour forth onto the surface, and the area around the forest of ships became a hubbub of activity as ranks were formed, heavy weapons unloaded. . . .

"Now!" Robert Ching cried aloud. He threw the switch.

Ching immediately transferred his attention to the viewscreen showing the top of the landing pit. The doors began to slide open . . . the crack widened. . . . And now the doors were at full-open position, and the screen showed the *Prometheus* sitting at the bottom of the pit with only naked space above it. . . .

In the control room of the *Prometheus,* Boris Johnson, cradled in his Cocoon, stared at a viewscreen in evergrowing confusion as he watched the Hegemonic ships land. *Somehow,* Robert Ching had gotten them to come down. Duntov would be able to lift the *Prometheus,* perhaps get clear of the asteroid. . . .

But it all seemed so pointless. They might get as much as a five minute head start on the Hegemonic ships before the Commander of the flotilla realized what was happening. But what good would it do them? They could have five *hours'* lead on the Hegemonic ships, and the cruisers would still be able to overtake the *Prometheus* and blast it into a million pieces. . . .

Confusedly, half-cursing the small glimmer of hope that still flickered within him, Johnson turned his attention to the viewscreen showing the massive doors above the landing pit. And as he watched, the doors began to slide open, smoothly, inexorably. . . .

And the stars shone down clear and beckoning above the *Prometheus*.

"Well here goes nothing. . . ." Arkady Duntov said wanly. He cut in the anti-gravs.

Johnson felt a momentary floating sensation as the anti-gravs neutralized both the artificial gravity of the base installations and the near negligible natural gravity of the asteroid itself.

Then he was crushed back into his Cocoon as the main reaction drive cut in at full emergency power, and the *Prometheus* bolted upward, past the rock walls of the pit, and out into the cold, black, free space.

As the tremendous acceleration weighted his body, Johnson kept his eyes glued on the benign panorama of space on the forward facing viewscreen, not daring to gaze upon that which filled his mind—the Hegemonic ships which even now must be spotting the *Prometheus,* running through hasty countdown cycles, lifting off in swift, deadly pursuit. . . .

While the *Prometheus* accelerated outward, starward, Johnson stolidly steeled himself for the shock that must soon come, as the Hegemonic ships attacked, with lasecannon, with thermonuclear missiles. . . . He wondered morbidly if he would even have time to feel the shock before the *Prometheus* was atomized. . . .

As the *Prometheus* reached for the stars, Boris Johnson waited for the death that he expected to come at any moment, waited for the fatal blow that surely must fall. . . . He waited and waited and waited. . . .

The great starship leaping up out of the landing pit seemed to Robert Ching the greatest sight he had ever seen, the culmination, the fulfillment of his whole life. His soul seemed to leap up with it as the *Prometheus* reached for the stars, for the future of man.

A future, Ching vowed, that will not be denied. Mentally, he began counting off the seconds until the second switch could safely be thrown . . . ten . . . fifteen . . . thirty. . . .

With a wrenching mental effort, Ching tore his eyes away from the sight of the *Prometheus* and focused his attention on the second viewscreen, which showed the Hegemonic ships.

Apparently, they had already spotted the *Prometheus,* for confusion reigned amidst the forest of ships. Some airlocks were already shut, some ships were hastily reloading troops, other Guards were milling about aimlessly. . . .

One minute . . . a minute and ten seconds . . . a minute and fifteen seconds. . . .

Ching glanced around at the assembled Brothers. All were watching the viewscreen, and he saw many pairs of lips moving as they mentally counted with him.

Two minutes and ten seconds . . . twenty . . . thirty . . . forty. . . .

Robert Ching hesitated for the briefest moment, blinked his eyes, and threw the second switch on the control panel.

Deep within the bowels of the asteroid, surrounded by tons of lead shielding, a signal reached the automatic control system of the Brotherhood headquarters' nuclear reactor. One by one, and then in whole clusters, dampening rods began to withdraw from the reactor, and the reaction mass within raced toward critical, toward that moment of titanic nuclear explosion which would blast the asteroid and all on or in it—Brothers, Guards, Hegemonic ships—to atoms.

The great nuclear explosion that would destroy every Hegemonic ship and clear the path to the stars.

Victory through suicide—the Ultimate Chaotic Act.

Robert Ching turned to stare at the stars, at the vastness of space with which the great all-encompassing viewscreen in which he floated surrounded him. Over the heads of the watching Brothers, each man facing this moment alone and silent, he saw the tiny silver streak that was the *Prometheus,* hurtling towards the images of the stars on the great viewscreen before him.

Ching blinked his eyes, and to him it was as if the viewscreen that surrounded him was reality itself. . . .

He was floating free in space, one with the universe in which he was but a mote, the millions upon millions of stars, each a warming sun, on and on and on, without end, infinitely, Chaotically—the destiny of Man.

In his mind's eye, the moment of destruction that raced towards him was already upon him. . . . The asteroid, the Hegemonic ships, the substance of his own body, rendered by the nuclear fire to the primal Chaos from which they had coalesced. . . . His mind, his thoughts, his being, his ego, not simply destroyed but disintegrated, Randomized, one with the Chaotic universe. . . .

And his last thought, as anticipation became reality, as asteroid, ships, men, and Robert Ching, First Agent of the Brotherhood of Assassins, were vaporized, was one of utter mystic ecstasy, as he savored his death even as it happened— a death with victory, a death that united him, body and mind, with that which he had served.

Robert Ching was at last one with Chaos.

Boris Johnson suddenly felt a great shudder go through the hull of the *Prometheus*, jarring his bones even through the stress-fiber packing of the Gee-Cocoon.

As it happened, he fully expected the ship to split open or another near miss to occur, or to be instantly erased forever as the *Prometheus* was vaporized by a direct hit.

But none of these things happened. Instead, he half-heard, half-felt the sounds of many small concussions against the outer hull, as if the ship were passing through some impossibly dense swarm of meteors.

Then . . . *nothing!* No further concussions, no more sounds, no moment of searing nuclear fire. Nothing. They . . . they were alive.

He glanced up at the viewscreen showing the view forward of the ship—stars and blackness, nothing more.

"What was that?" he finally grunted.

"I don't know," Duntov said. "Unless. . . ."

Johnson saw him reach out, activate the rear-facing viewscreen camera. The viewscreen came to life, and Johnson looked for the asteroid and the Hegemonic flotilla which by now certainly must be pursuing them. . . .

But neither were there. Where the asteroid and the ships should've been, he saw nothing but an expanding cloud of dust and debris, flotsam so fine it seemed like no more than gravel. That was what he had felt. The asteroid exploding and bits of metal and rock rattling off the hull. Asteroid and ships alike were now dust. And all those men. . . .

But the Prometheus now was safe.

Then Johnson felt himself float weightless as Duntov cut off the reaction drive.

"What act can be more truly Chaotic than Victory through suicide. . . ?" Arkady Duntov whispered.

"What?"

"A quote from Markowitz," Duntov said. "Something about what he called the 'Ultimate Chaotic Act.' Victory through suicide."

"You mean . . . you mean you think it wasn't an accident?" Johnson said. "Ching blew up the asteroid on purpose?"

"I'm sure of it," Duntov said. "They gave their lives to destroy the Hegemonic ships. They sacrificed themselves so the *Prometheus* could go to the stars."

Boris Johnson understood and did not understand. It was something a coldly logical man, a Gorov, might've done, a ruthlessly logical weighing of their own lives against the future of the human race. But somehow, viscerally, he suspected that there had been nothing cold about it.

And he sensed that, for Robert Ching, it had not been an act of bleak desperation, but something else, something that had meaning in a way he could never understand. Johnson shivered. The Millennium of Religion was supposed to have died centuries ago. Had it died now with Robert Ching? He wondered . . . would it ever die?

And an hour later, when the final course corrections had been made and the *Prometheus* was irrevocably on its way to 61 Cygnus, Boris Johnson stared in wonder at the far stars to which they would soon be hurtling at many times the speed of light.

He looked at the stars, and only now, with the Hegemony and the dangers he had traversed to reach this moment receding behind him, did he realize that nothing was over, that it all was really just beginning.

What was out there? Star after star, race after race, danger after danger, without end in time or space. Racial immortality for Man, perhaps, but an immortality that he would have to wrest from an indifferent universe again and again and again.

The struggle was just beginning. In another billion years, it would still be just beginning. It would always be beginning.

Boris Johnson, frail mote of temporarily reversed entropy, looked upon the billions of stars stretched before him, islands in an infinite ocean without bottom, without shore, without end—and looked squarely for the first time in his life upon the countenance of Chaos.

And it seemed to him, that in those unwinking stars, the myriad blind eyes of Chaos, the scattered atoms that had once been the face of Robert Ching stared back.